# Blind Date

All morning long, Fiona continued to hope that Jonathan wouldn't show up. But at the stroke of noon, the doorbell rang twice. Fiona grimaced at her reflection in the hall mirror, brushed a fleck of mascara off her cheek, and hurried down the hall. She paused with one hand on the doorknob and took a deep breath. She didn't want Jonathan to get the idea that she was the least bit nervous about this idiotic blind date. She promised herself, one last time, to be nice to Jeremy's friend — no matter how boring and difficult the afternoon turned out to be.

She flung open the door, and suddenly she forgot her carefully prepared introduction. Fiona found herself looking way up at a tall guy, straight into a pair of startlingly penetrating gray eyes. He didn't look the least bit like the Hollywood hero Jeremy had described. He looked more like the David Bowie poster Fiona had over her bed, even though he *was* wearing a soft Indiana Jones-style hat. The gray felt made his eyes seem even grayer.

Books from Scholastic
in the **Couples** series:

# DANCE WITH ME

### by M.E. Cooper

SCHOLASTIC INC.
New York Toronto London Auckland Sydney

ISBN 0-590-40240-4

12 11 10 9 8 7 6 5 4 3 2          0 1 2 3 4 5/9

Printed in the U.S.A.          01

First Scholastic printing, November 1986

# Chapter

# 1

It was a rainy day in late November, the kind of day Fiona Stone loved. The Maryland air was fresh and damp, and even though the Washington, D.C., suburb of Rose Hill was three hours from the shore, the breeze that blew through the open window of Fiona's bedroom held a hint of the sea in it.

Fiona sat on the window seat, her graceful neck arched back, her head propped against the wall. As she watched thick gray clouds float across the darkening sky, she decided the stormy weather matched her mood perfectly. She took a deep breath and closed her large blue eyes. It smelled, it *felt* just like home. On a day like today she could almost imagine being back in England, walking with her friends down the cliffside path that led to a scrap of beach below the stately stone buildings of Kingsmont Ballet Academy.

But her friends were thousands of miles away, and Fiona wasn't a student at Kingsmont anymore; she was a sophomore at Kennedy High. She tried to swallow the lump in her throat that had been there ever since she had left England in October and come to America to join the rest of the family. Her brother Jeremy and her parents had been in Rose Hill since August when her father was named cultural attaché at the British Embassy in Washington. Jeremy had been ecstatic about the move to the States; Fiona hadn't given it a second thought, because she didn't think she'd be going.

Fiona had stayed behind in London to audition for the National Ballet. Night after night before the audition, she had dreamed of falling flat on her face on the big Covent Garden stage, or blanking out on the choreography to her solo while company directors watched from the front row. But, even in her wildest nightmares, Fiona had never dreamed of not making it into the troupe. She had been dancing since she was six, and by the time she had graduated to Kingsmont's senior school, Fiona and her roommate had become the stars of the school. Everyone knew Fiona and Elizabeth would be the two young dancers the National Ballet would eventually "bring up" from the corps. The company always seemed to choose future ballerinas in pairs: one allegro, or fast-moving, petite dancer like Fiona; and one tall, lyrical adagio dancer like Lizzy.

Out of the ballet studio, dark-haired Lizzy always dressed and looked as remote and roman-

tic as she danced. Fiona was blonde and ener-
getic. Her feet seemed to move at the speed of
light, and her disposition was sunny and joyous,
even mischievous at times. Fiona and Lizzy were
best friends and they both seemed destined for
great things. Fiona never imagined herself not
dancing or not getting into the National Ballet —
if only as last girl in the back row of corps dancers
headed for a difficult, anonymous career.

She finally auditioned, and didn't fall, or miss a
step. Fiona felt like a star, skimming the surface
of the stage just like Margot Fonteyn, and other
greats. She wasn't prepared to fail; to be passed
over for a dancer with good technique but no style
or flair, to lose out, because she wasn't the right
type after all. But that was exactly what happened, and Fiona had gone straight home from
the Opera House and packed her bags. Her last
suitcase was almost full before reality hit home:
She was never going to dance at the National
Ballet. As far as Fiona was concerned, that
meant she wasn't going to dance for anyone. She
burst into tears, and cried for what seemed like
days. A numbness soon set in and by the time
Fiona boarded the plane to America, she was sure
of only two things: Her new life was beginning on
a pretty low note, and she never, ever wanted to
dance again.

Fiona drew up her slender legs on the window
cushion and massaged her temples with her
fingers. A funny pressure had been building up
behind her eyes for at least a week now. In spite
of her thick pink sweater and warm black leg-

gings, she shivered. But she didn't close the window. She rested her flushed cheek against the cool pane and watched a big blue van pull into the Rifkins' driveway across the street. Seconds later, Jeremy's friends Michael Rifkin and Phoebe Hall climbed out. As they headed into the big white house that resembled the Stones', Michael slung his arm around Phoebe's shoulder and tousled her long red hair. It was Thursday, the day that Phoebe had her singing lesson. Michael opened the front door and Phoebe's laugh drifted upward. Fiona bit her lip. Phoebe sounded so happy. Fiona wondered if *she'd* ever feel that good again. The Rifkins' door closed with a muffled bang, and Fiona pushed the window open even wider.

Miss Spinelli, Michael's mother and Phoebe's teacher, made her sing with the music room windows open, and Fiona loved hearing Phoebe's clear soprano voice. The songs Phoebe sang were beautiful, and some of them were the same Schubert tunes that the accompanist at Kingsmont had played in Fiona's ballet classes.

For six Thursday evenings now, Fiona had waited by her window, sitting perfectly still, just listening. Eventually Phoebe would begin her exercises and progress into her songs. Fiona would close her eyes and feel herself dancing again. She hadn't taken a ballet class for over six weeks — the longest time in her sixteen years she had spent away from the barre. The pressure behind her eyes suddenly gave way and she tried to choke back a sob.

4

"Fee Fi Fo Fum, I smell the blood of an Englishman." Jeremy Stone announced his arrival with a knock on his sister's half opened door. Fiona abruptly rubbed the tears from her eyes with the back of her hand, but not before Jeremy poked his head into her room and spotted her scrunched in the corner of the window seat, her complexion blotchy, and her eye makeup streaked.

A shadow crossed his handsome, angular face, as he asked awkwardly, "Uh — should I leave?"

Fiona shook her head and quickly closed the window. She kept her face down, and shoved her large overstuffed scrapbook under a pile of sweaters beside her on the window seat.

Jeremy leaned against the far wall, his camera dangling from his neck. He wore the baggy black wool jacket his girl friend Diana Einerson had found when they were rummaging in a Georgetown flea market for video props. His pockets bulged with film. As Fiona looked up into Jeremy's piercing blue-gray eyes, she thought he looked handsome enough to be a movie star. He had the same fine-boned features she did, but his eyes were smaller and his coloring darker. Jeremy's hair was straight and almost black. Like his sister, he was full of an intense pent-up energy, and seemed to be constantly in motion.

Jeremy looked around the room and said, "Looks like a tornado hit this place. It's enough to put anyone out of sorts." He grimaced, and unsnapped his camera case. He put the lens cap in his pocket and began scanning the room through his viewfinder. Jeremy looked up quickly and wiggled his dark eyebrows. "Don't mind me. I'm just the local insurance investigator. Need pics for the damage report," he said in his clipped British accent.

In spite of her mood, Fiona found herself smiling. Jeremy was such a clown sometimes. The best — no, the *only* good thing about coming to America was the chance to get to know her brother better. Except for holidays, Fiona had spent practically her whole life away at ballet boarding school. Jeremy had lived at home with their parents, and moved around the world with them on Mr. Stone's various diplomatic assignments. As a result, Jeremy had missed a year of school.

Nevertheless, Fiona felt an odd sort of closeness to Jeremy. He was her only brother, and less than a year and a half older than she. But Jeremy didn't seem to know the slightest bit about her: what she liked to do or wear, what her favorite bands were, or how she really thought about things. Maybe now he'd stop giving her predictable "my little sister the ballerina" presents, like her silly ballerina jewelry box. Fiona had hated it the moment she saw it. But now she'd never part with it. Jeremy had bought it for her when she was twelve and went off to Kingsmont senior school on scholarship.

"There's not very much to investigate, sir," Fiona tried to joke. "My trunk, which has been lost at sea for six whole weeks now, finally arrived. I'm unpacking." She gestured toward the four-poster bed heaped with sweaters, scarves, and underwear, then stood up and stretched. Fiona flopped forward and dangled with her head almost brushing the floor. Her pink bandanna slipped low on her forehead, and after she slowly rolled herself up to a standing position again, Fiona tore it from her hair and tossed it onto a a white wicker chair. She shook her short hair loose and glanced around the room. Jeremy was right — it did look like a major catastrophe had struck. Unpacking her trunk had turned her high-ceilinged room into a disaster area. Clothes spilled out of the dresser drawers, the closets were half full, and hangers littered the bed and chairs. Books and magazines were stacked on top of cartons. Her desk was littered with tapes and record albums. Bits of pink and white tulle peeped over the edge of the open black metal-edged trunk, and a plastic bag filled with toe shoes was lying against the base of a wall-sized mirror-and-practice barre Fiona's father had installed before she had arrived from England.

Jeremy focused his camera on a pile of shoes Fiona had left in the center of the room and began snapping pictures of them.

"Hey, what are you taking pictures of?" Fiona looked at Jeremy as if he were crazy.

"Doc Bartoly's still life assignment. He wants twenty photos of ordinary objects in a new and different setting. Your shoes fit the bill perfectly." Jeremy abruptly turned and aimed the camera at his sister.

Fiona's eyebrows arched in protest. Outside of

7

Jeremy's new girl friend, Fiona was his favorite model. She was totally at ease in front of the camera. Fiona struck a pretty pose for her brother, then a goofy one. She grabbed a straw hat from a hook on the wall, and twisted her face into a silly smile.

"That's more like it. You were looking a bit tragic when I walked in," Jeremy said. Fiona looked away quickly, and began putting away her things.

Jeremy followed her around the room, snapping pictures from different angles as he talked. "Actually, about feeling tragic — "

"I'm not feeling tragic," Fiona interrupted, her arms full of skirts. "I was listening to Phoebe Hall sing. The song was sad, and I always cry at sad songs."

"Ah, Phoebe was singing." Jeremy marched over to the window. A path of light streamed out of the music room windows at Michael's house. Jeremy considered taking a picture, then changed his mind. He snapped the lens cap back on, and flopped down onto the bright pillows in a wicker easy chair. "Phoebe and singing are not unrelated to why I came knocking at your door." He leaned forward, with his elbows on his knees, and regarded his sister intently. A concerned look flickered across his face. "So you've been at school about a month now," he began, imitating the flat American accent of a popular radio talkshow host. "What's your opinion of life at Kennedy High, Ms. Stone? The truth please."

Fiona gave him a puzzled look. "What do I

think of Kennedy?" she repeated. She sank down gracefully onto the polished oak floor, and absently fingered a white shag rug half hanging out of her trunk. "Actually I haven't really thought about Kennedy at all," she admitted. Jeremy looked skeptical. "Really!" she insisted. "But since you asked, I guess I'd give it mixed reviews."

Jeremy frowned. "Mixed reviews?" He focused his camera across the room on Fiona's reflection in the wall-to-wall mirror.

"Some things are okay, some aren't," Fiona said tensely. This conversation was beginning to make her nervous. Jeremy was in one of his scheming moods. Fiona had only been around him a few weeks, but she could tell when he was up to something.

Jeremy nodded thoughtfully, then asked, "What's the good part of life at Kennedy? What's the bad? Maybe Sasha Jenkins can publish your critique in *The Red and the Gold*. It could be a new column: Brit Crit."

"Very funny." Fiona wrinkled her nose in distaste. She wasn't sure she could think of anything good about Kennedy. It seemed like a nice place, but she didn't really want to be there. But Fiona knew the bad she was feeling inside had nothing to do with Kennedy either. Or did it? Suddenly she wasn't sure. Maybe part of it had to do with the students. Or the fact that Kennedy was so big. Kingsmont was a small, intimate school where Fiona had known everyone. In spite of Jeremy's attempts to include her in his crowd at Kennedy,

Fiona felt like an outsider for the first time in her life. American teenagers were so different than her friends back home. They were louder, more boisterous, and much too interested in having a good time. There was a general free-spirited atmosphere around the Kennedy quad that Fiona liked, but she felt a little uncomfortable with it, too. She couldn't exactly say what it was, but something was definitely missing.

Until six weeks ago, all of Fiona's classmates and friends had been dancers. Jeremy's group of friends were among the most attractive kids in school. They did lots of interesting things: Chris Austin was student body president, Woody Webster ran all sorts of theater and drama projects, Sasha was editor of the paper, and Peter Lacey ran the on-campus radio station, WKND. They were all very nice people, but none of them knew what it was like to live only for the ballet.

Jeremy cleared his throat, and Fiona jumped slightly. She had almost forgotten he was there, rewinding his camera, waiting for her to answer his question.

"Forget about the bad, for a minute. I bet Dee Patterson's a good part," Jeremy prompted.

Fiona nodded vigorously, and for the first time that afternoon her delicate features lit up. "Dee's great. I can't believe I've made such a good friend already. I just met her a month ago and I feel like I know her as well as Lizzy."

Fiona sat back on her heels and toyed with the single plastic earring that dangled from her right ear. Meeting Dee at dancercise class had been the high point of Fiona's first few weeks at school. Fiona had actually introduced Dee to the kids she herself had just met in Jeremy's crowd. Just recently, Dee had started dating one of them, Marc Harrison. Bubbly, friendly Dee fit in perfectly with the group, while Fiona remained on the fringe.

"Well, I bet if you signed up for more activities around school, you'd meet a lot of terrific kids like Dee — you'd even get to know the kids you've met already better."

Fiona eyed Jeremy suspiciously as he leaped to his feet and enthusiastically began pacing the floor. "And the perfect thing's come up, Fiona. The Kennedy Players have been rehearsing a holiday production of *Oklahoma!* for a couple of weeks now. But they need dancers. In fact they're *desperate* for dancers. Woody Webster told me so himself. They've been auditioning all week. Tomorrow's the last day for tryouts."

At the mention of the word "audition," Fiona's shoulders tightened. She stared at her brother in disbelief. "You want *me* to try out for a school production of a musical?" She dismissed Jeremy with a vague wave of her hand. "You're off, Jeremy. I can't sing. I don't know the first thing about musicals. Can't even say I like them." She spoke very quickly and her voice had a hard edge to it. Fiona rolled and unrolled the same pair of pink tights three times before tossing them into an open drawer. "Besides, I'm having enough trouble keeping up with all the school work — "

"Trouble?" Jeremy scoffed. "You started the

11

semester nearly two months late, and you're practically getting straight A's. You're headed for the honor society, like it or not. In fact, I think something other than school work is just what you need. You're studying way too much."

Fiona caught her breath. She swallowed hard, and forced herself to sound calm. "Okay, so I already study too much. You're probably right," she conceded. "But I don't know why I'm bothering to make up excuses. The point is, Jeremy, I'm not interested in dancing right now, and I'm certainly not interested in *Oklahoma!* Kennedy is a big enough school that Woody should be able to find plenty of decent dancers."

Jeremy looked up at the ceiling and groaned under his breath. "Fiona," he pleaded patiently, "Would you listen, for once? This isn't just a school musical. It's one of the greatest pieces of American musical theater. Half the show is ballet. You wouldn't have to sing a note. Or say a word. And it's being done for a good cause. All proceeds from ticket sales go to the Holiday Drive for the Homeless. Woody's trying to put on an extra special show this time around."

Fiona gnawed her lower lip. Her voice shook slightly as she said, "Jeremy, the point is, I'm not a theatrical dancer. I'm a ballet dancer. That's all I know how to do. Dramatic musicals just aren't my style. Even the ones I like, I wouldn't feel comfortable dancing in. I think — I'm not sure — but I think *Oklahoma!* is one I definitely don't like. It's the one about cowboys, right?"

Jeremy started to protest, but then spotted

Fiona's face. Two little red spots burned in each cheek, and her full lips were drawn into a tight, thin line. He suddenly wasn't sure if she was going to yell at him or burst into tears. He shook his head and sauntered over to the door. "Just thought I'd let you know about the tryouts. Didn't mean to make such a big deal about it." He stopped before walking into the hall. "I'm going to Diana's to study after dinner. French quiz tomorrow. Want to meet us at the sub shop later?"

Fiona shook her head. She liked Diana a lot but she felt uncomfortable always tagging along with the two of them. Besides, Jeremy's suggestion about the audition had unnerved her. She wanted to finish cleaning her room, then crawl into bed and just be alone.

Jeremy headed down the hall, then paused outside his room. "I guess I just want to see you have more fun here, Fiona. I know you didn't exactly plan to move to the States, but Kennedy's a really great place. I thought the play would be a good way to get into the swing of things. Besides, I think the Players could use you."

"Jeremy," Fiona started tightly, then softened her tone. "I know you meant well by all this. But don't worry so much about me. I'll be okay."

She stepped back into her room and shut the door, then leaned against it and closed her eyes. Why was it so hard to tell the truth, to talk about how she really felt about dancing? The only person who understood was Lizzy, and she was a million miles away.

She certainly couldn't talk to Jeremy or her

parents about ballet. She felt she had somehow let them down when she didn't get into the National Ballet — especially Jeremy. He seemed to have such crazy expectations of her, as if she could do anything she set her mind to. Fiona knew she was a determined person. But she had been determined to be a great ballerina and found that determination and hard work hadn't been enough. Now she felt like she never wanted to dance again, but the truth was she was scared to death of even trying.

Fiona hugged her long thin arms around her body and thought of how she had just lied to her brother. She should have told him the truth. Even if she truly wanted to try out for *Oklahoma!*, she couldn't muster up the courage. She couldn't bear the humiliation of not being good enough for a high school musical. That was the real reason she told Jeremy to count her out.

Fiona sank down on the edge of her bed and stared blankly at her trunk. A second later she focused on the pink tulle of her graduation performance tutu poking stiffly over the edge. Her cheeks flushed with anger. She yanked the pink sequinned skirt out and started to pull at it. She wanted to tear it apart, throw it away. But the seams were well-sewn and strong; it didn't tear easily. After a few pulls, she let her hands drop into her lap. She stared miserably at the lovely costume. She had worn it to dance Princess Aurora's Rose Adagio in *Sleeping Beauty*. Never in the history of Kingsmont had the girl lead in the graduation performance not made it into the

National Ballet. Fiona crushed the dress to her and threw herself face down on the bed. The sequin and tulle scratched her face as she burst into tears again. But Fiona didn't care. Never in her life had she felt so humiliated, so lost, and so alone.

# Chapter
# 2

"*A demain, mon ami?*" Diana Einerson looked across the kitchen table at Jeremy. His chin was propped in his hands and he was staring blankly at the bulletin board next to the refrigerator. His toe tapped a nervous rhythm on the kitchen floor and, for the fourth time in ten minutes, he heaved a sigh. "Jeremy?" she prodded gently, and reached across the yellow Formica tabletop to take his hand.

"Sorry," Jeremy apologized, running his long fingers through his dark hair. "I mean, *pardon*. What were we up to? I sort of lost track of things." He caught the glint in Diana's wide brown eyes and defended himself quickly. "Come on, Diana, I don't know how to say all that in French." They had solemnly promised each other that if they studied together for the French quiz they would only speak French, even if they

16

weren't talking about the lesson.

"Jeremy, if my company bores you so much. . . ." Diana feigned a hurt expression.

"Oh, Di, stop it. You know it's not the company that bores me. I'm not bored, I'm mixed up. I don't know." Jeremy tilted his chair back and stuffed his hands in the pockets of his jeans. "I just feel all cooped up in here right now. I want to get out, do something. Anything but study French. And I want to be with you. You know that."

"We have exactly two more lines of our French dialogue to memorize. Actually you just have to say, 'I'll see you tomorrow' in French." Diana planted her elbows on the table and tried to look stern.

Jeremy folded his hands in front of him on the table, a smile playing at the corners of his mouth. "*A demain, ma cherie, en francais.* That's it, isn't it: 'Until tomorrow, my dear, in French'?"

"Jeremy, did anyone ever tell you you're exasperating?" Diana groaned and closed her notebook. She stuffed it in her book bag and pulled out a rubber band, then gathered her long blonde hair into a high ponytail.

"Who, me?" Jeremy sounded very surprised. "No. No one's ever said that."

Diana yanked the elastic around her hair a couple of more times. "Well, you are. It's extremely frustrating studying with you. We have a major quiz tomorrow at nine-fifteen AM and you act like you don't know the first thing about French. You've studied it since you were a kid.

17

Why do you think I picked you for a partner in class?"

Jeremy considered Diana thoughtfully. He scratched his head and said in his best cowboy accent, "Oh, I reckon because I'm the guy you've been going out with for two months now." He ended up sounding more like Diana's brother, Bart, than John Wayne. He jumped up from the table and in two steps was by Diana's side. "Tell me it's so, darling!" He pulled Diana to her feet and gave her a loud smacking kiss.

Diana pretended to struggle, then went limp in his arms. She conceded, "Okay, you win. It's true. I picked you as a French partner because I get to see you in the middle of the week that way." She circled his neck with her arms, and leaned back to look into his face. "But if my grades suffer, my father's going to catch on."

Jeremy smiled, and traced the outline of her face with his finger. He drew Diana closer and brushed her lips lightly with his own. Her arms tightened around his neck. They were still enjoying their kiss when Bart clunked down the stairs and into the kitchen.

"Now that's what I call studying French!" Bart teased, spotting the couple still entwined by the kitchen table. "Hope I'm not interrupting something." He laughed as Jeremy and Diana hastily broke apart. Diana blushed and began rearranging her ponytail. Bart punched Jeremy playfully on the shoulder as he headed for the refrigerator. The broad-shouldered football player opened the door and stared glumly at the picked-over remains

18

of a turkey. He chose the container of milk instead, and offered some to Jeremy. "You guys still studying?"

Jeremy reached for his jacket and replied, "We just finished the last line of our dialogue, and were heading for the sub shop. Want to come? Is Holly back yet?" Jeremy asked. Bart's girl friend had gone to a science fair in New York with the other chemistry honor students.

"She's getting in late tonight," Bart said. "I'm getting cabin fever around here but I can't go *anywhere*. You're not the only ones with a test tomorrow. Mr. Ryan's got us memorizing all these dumb Shakespeare sonnets. I'll be up all night and I've got rehearsals for the show after school. You could bring me home a sub though, but make it — "

"Anything but turkey!" Diana finished the sentence for her brother. She pulled her denim jacket off the hook and wrapped a bright plaid scarf around her neck. "We won't be too long, Bart," she added as she and Jeremy headed out the door.

Jeremy drew her hand through his arm as he led her to the car. "Sorry I let my mind wander during our French lesson," he said. "I'm feeling restless, and it's got nothing to do with French."

"Is it Fiona?" she asked as they climbed into Jeremy's rusty old Saab.

Jeremy leaned his forehead against the steering wheel and said, "She's so down these days. All the life's gone out of her," he said flatly. "Di, you would have loved her if you'd met her before that dreadful audition. She was so magical, so alive. Now she's kind of dug herself a hole and is hiding in it."

Diana frowned slightly. "Jeremy, it makes sense, you know. Just think how disappointing that kind of experience must be. And then, with no time to recover, she had to move here, just like that." Diana snapped her fingers and gave a little shudder. "I think she's had a pretty rough time of it lately. She doesn't seem so bad, considering. I mean, she keeps to herself a lot, but that's only natural. This is a new place."

Jeremy shook his head and rapped his fingers nervously against the steering wheel as they pulled into the traffic on Rosemont Boulevard. "Of course, she's disappointed. I can understand that. But that doesn't bother me half as much as the way she's stopped dancing completely. Do you realize she hasn't taken one dance class — except for that dancercise stuff — since the day of the audition? Real dancers don't do that. Fiona never missed a class in her life. I thought she'd get here and enroll at the Academy of Ballet Arts in Georgetown. She's just sixteen. She shouldn't be giving up so easily."

Diana didn't know what to say. She glanced at Jeremy. He seemed preoccupied, edgy, as if he was mulling something over in his head. Diana lightly rested her hand on his arm.

They rode in silence the rest of the way to the sub shop. Jeremy turned off the ignition but didn't make a move to get out of the car. He closed his eyes and leaned against the headrest. "My parents have been real low-key about it. They think it's better to leave her alone. I thought at first that was a good idea, but not talking about it isn't helping her, either. Fiona needs to get out and do things — be with people. If she isn't going to dance again, she's got to find a new life. It's understandable for her to be so devastated, but I think it's time she started getting over it. I just wish I could think of something to do that would help. I told her about Woody needing dancers for *Oklahoma!*"

"Jeremy, that's a great idea! Woody needs a choreographer, too, and Fiona would be perfect. She could help him pull the show together. I bet she has lots of experience performing."

"Yeah, and it would be the perfect way for her to get involved in things around Kennedy. But try telling Fiona that. She won't have the first thing to do with it. She won't even go to the auditions."

"Of course not," Diana said promptly.

"What do you mean?" Jeremy asked, startled. "She just failed one audition."

"She didn't *fail*. They told her to try again next year. They just needed a dancer with a different style, that's all. But it was a crummy break, and it really threw Fiona. She didn't fail."

Diana arched her eyebrows. "I know that. So do you. But she feels like she bombed. It's just too soon. Give her time, Jeremy. Have some confidence in her. She'll come around soon enough. She's so new here." Diana cuddled up close to Jeremy, and took his hand between both of hers.

"So am I. So are you," Jeremy noted.

Diana dropped his hand and said slowly, "Some people have more trouble adjusting to change than others. Fiona's not used to new places. When my family moved to Rose Hill, Bart did really well at first. He made friends practically the minute we walked in the door. Leaving Montana was the hardest thing I'd ever done, and I really had a tough time the first few weeks. Everything seemed to go wrong. I made some pretty big mistakes," Diana admitted.

"I hope I wasn't one of them," Jeremy joked. He turned Diana's face toward his and waited for her reaction.

Diana burst out laughing. "Jeremy Stone, you're what made all the mistakes not matter so much. When you turned up, all my troubles vanished." Diana entwined her fingers through Jeremy's.

He leaned toward her and was about to kiss her when he sat up straight and cried out, "I've got it, Di! I've got it. How could I have been so dumb?"

Diana eyed him suspiciously.

"A boyfriend," he said smugly. "That's what she needs. A guy. I'll fix her up with a guy. I know I'm prejudiced — but I think she really is one of the two most beautiful girls in the school." He paused long enough to kiss Diana on the tip of her nose. "Any guy would love to date her."

Diana pulled back and shook her head. "Jeremy," she warned, "I don't think a guy is what Fiona needs right now. I mean, she's still pretty upset about dancing and everything. I can't picture her in a relationship yet." Diana fished for ammunition to dissuade Jeremy. "It's always better when two people find each other on their own. Like we did. She is beautiful, and lots of guys notice her when she walks around the halls. I'm sure Fiona will find someone to date when she's ready."

Jeremy wasn't listening. "But who?" he mumbled, opening the car door. As he started across the lot to the sub shop, he said, more to himself than Diana, "All the guys I know well are seeing people."

"Except Ted," Diana said with a resigned sigh. Jeremy had blinders on. Nothing was going to change his mind about finding someone for his sister.

"Ted!" Jeremy shouted gleefully, then dropped his voice to a conspiratorial whisper. "He's perfect. He's good-looking, extremely nice, and unattached."

"Jeremy, wake up." Diana stopped and forced Jeremy to face her. "You're getting carried away with this. Ted's still hung up on the girl he met this summer. Remember? Phoebe told us about it at Sasha's Halloween party. He's not ready for someone else."

"Too bad. He's such a nice guy." Jeremy sounded really disappointed. He laced his fingers through Diana's and led them toward the sub shop. "But there's got to be someone," he insisted. "Someone just right for her, someone like you for me and me for you." He pulled Diana toward him, and gazed earnestly into her eyes. "Meeting you made my wildest, craziest dreams about America somehow come true. I just want my kid sister to be this happy, too," he whispered.

Sensible words of protest about blind dates and playing matchmaker died on Diana's lips as Jeremy sealed them with a kiss.

# Chapter
# 3

"Hey, Stone, over here!" Peter Lacey, Kennedy High's DJ, shouted over the Springsteen song blaring from the sub shop jukebox. He motioned Jeremy and Diana over toward the crowd's favorite spot: the much-coveted corner booth. Monica Ford and Sasha Jenkins were already seated around the old wooden table. They greeted the couple warmly as they walked up.

"I thought Monsieur D'Etard was giving a major quiz tomorrow," Sasha said, sliding over to make room for Diana.

"You'd better believe it!" Diana groaned, taking off her jacket and tucking her pegged jeans more snugly into the tops of her cowboy boots. "Looks like we weren't the only ones who finished studying early." She glanced around the crowded Kennedy hangout. Kennedy pennants decorated the walls, and an old beat up motorcycle was suspended over the self-service counter. The place was packed and unusually lively for a school night.

"To think, Di, we planned on an intimate evening dining alone!" Jeremy laughed when he returned from the counter with a tray of Cokes and subs.

"Romeo here thinks he's got problems!" Monica sniffed and lightly punched her cousin Jeremy's arm. "I'll have you know we came here to have a private business meeting about the future of WKND!" Monica tossed her shiny hair off her face and grimaced at the noisy crowd. "We might as well have met in the middle of the cafeteria during second period lunch!" Monica was Peter's assistant at Kennedy's on-campus radio station and she shared the airwaves with him during the noon music show. She was also his girl friend.

"What's happening to WKND?" Jeremy asked, as he handed Diana her Coke and an order of fries, and bit into his own Super Salami Sinker Sub.

"Nothing," Monica continued. "We're trying to figure out some new and interesting possibilities for the future, though. Peter won't be at Kennedy forever."

"What's happening to Peter?" Greg Montgomery came up to the table, and squeezed in next to Jeremy. He took off his "I Sailed Chesapeake Bay" cap, and tossed it across the room. It landed right on the head of a dusty, stuffed polar bear off in a corner by the jukebox. Sasha winced. She couldn't stand looking at the sub shop mascot, especially when she was eating.

"Nice shot!" Peter congratulated the tall, lanky sophomore. Like Jeremy and Diana, Greg was fairly new to the crowd. He had started going with Chris Austin at the end of the summer, and even though he was the youngest member of the group, he was already well-known as one of the really active students on the Kennedy scene.

"Has anybody seen Chris?" Greg asked, glancing up at the antique Pepsi-Cola clock on the wall. "I'm supposed to meet her here." The words were scarcely out of his mouth when a pair of hands reached out from behind him and covered his eyes.

"Guess who?" said a warm, throaty voice.

Greg screwed up his face. "Sounds like an Austin."

"Which Austin?" two voices asked at once.

Greg touched the hands over his eyes. A happy smile lit up his face. "Chris, who sounds like Brenda for some reason."

Chris Austin leaned over his shoulder, her long blonde braid swinging forward and brushing his cheek. She took away her hands, and laughed as she declared, "You're right on both counts!" She tossed her blue shoulder bag on the table and plopped herself down in his lap. Her stepsister Brenda walked up behind her, followed by a tall gray-eyed boy. A soft felt Indiana Jones-type hat was shoved back on his dark blond hair. He smiled and stood slightly back from the booth, his hands stuffed into the pockets of his jacket.

"Preston! What brings you here?" Jeremy jumped up and greeted the boy warmly. He pulled a couple of chairs up to the end of the table and turned toward Diana. "This is Diana Einerson. Di, Jonathan Preston — Kennedy's new student activities director. He's the chap I'm working with on setting up next semester's multiclub, multimedia video event."

Jonathan pulled off his long red and gold Kennedy scarf, and shook Diana's hand. "Einerson?" His soft gray eyes narrowed thoughtfully. "You and your brother Bart just got here from Montana, right?"

Diana nodded yes, surprised he had heard of her, though Bart was something of a football hero and already well-known around the school.

"How'd things go at Garfield House?" Greg asked Brenda.

She laughed and gestured toward Jonathan. "Ask him! He knocked the socks off Tony Martinez. And Martinez is a pretty tough guy to impress. One meeting with Jonathan and he's ready to donate every available broom closet in Garfield to storing canned beans for the homeless." She fingered her long dark hair thoughtfully. "Actually, Jonathan got Tony to thinking about housing the homeless."

"At Garfield?" Sasha asked.

"No," Chris replied. "Garfield's a halfway house for teens and it should stay that way."

Jonathan vigorously nodded in agreement. He put his chair down and leaned his elbows on the table. "Tony really knows how to get things done. I've never met anyone like him." He whistled in admiration. "And he's got all the right connections, a great success record, and so any suggestions he might make about starting a homeless center might be taken seriously. At least with Tony we've got a chance. Do you realize he's going to let us use the whole basement of Garfield House as a food distribution center once the contributions start coming in? He's even going to form a work crew with kids from the house. He's a real inspiration."

Jonathan greedily eyed the remains of Jeremy's sub. "Which reminds me, I'm starved. I could go for one of those Heroic Hollywood Ham subs." He got up and headed for the counter. "Brenda, Chris, want anything?" Both girls shook their heads.

"Jonathan's idea about proceeds from all extracurricular activities going to the Holiday Drive is a great one, and most of the kids are really enthusiastic about it, and willing to help. But I've heard the Kennedy Players are in trouble," Chris said. "Woody told me today only six kids showed up for the dance tryouts. I thought his plea at the assembly last Thursday would have moved the Lincoln Memorial into auditioning."

"What about Fiona?" Sasha asked Jeremy. "She's a *real* dancer."

Jeremy and Diana exchanged a glance. "Not interested, I guess," Jeremy said.

Until Sasha mentioned his sister, Jeremy had

29

almost forgotten about his plan to find Fiona a boyfriend. He sat back in his chair and watched Greg and Chris. They certainly seemed happy together. So did Monica and Peter. Looking around the table, Jeremy was more convinced than ever. Fiona would definitely be happier and feel more like she belonged if she met the right guy. Feeling loved might help her get over whatever problems she was having about dancing.

Jeremy's eyes rested on Jonathan. He was in the middle of a friendly argument with Peter and Sasha about how to best use the additional airtime soon to be granted to WKND. Jeremy wondered if Jonathan had a girl friend. He had a terrible way of forgetting these important details about his new friends. He sat forward in his seat and listened intently as Monica said, "Speaking of medieval music, I don't remember seeing you and Nicole at the Homecoming Dance." Nicole Peterson played lute in Kennedy's Early Music Ensemble, and Monica had interviewed the sophomore on her once-a-month live music program at WKND.

The constant smile faded from Jonathan's lips. He studied his hands a minute then shrugged. "Yeah — well — we split up right before the dance."

Monica winced. "Sorry, I didn't know," she mumbled.

"Aw, it's okay," Jonathan said. "She met a contra-bass player from Carrolton Academy. I think they have more in common. I can't say I like early music all that much," he confessed. Jeremy cocked his head and regarded Jonathan more intently. Jonathan and Fiona. He ran the names together in his head. The sound appealed to him.

After Jonathan's declaration, an awkward silence fell over the table. Chris checked her watch and cleared her throat. "Wow, Brenda, we've got to get home or we're going to be grounded." She looked first at Jonathan then Greg. "I know you both need a lift — "

"What's wrong with your car?" Jeremy asked Jonathan.

Jonathan shrugged sheepishly. The smile was back on his face again, but he still looked a little subdued. "Big Pink's on the blink — again. My friend Matt says she'll be fixed up in time for the weekend. Meanwhile — " he said, shoving his chair back and getting up to follow Chris, Greg, and Brenda toward the door.

"Hey, wait up. Diana only lives a couple of blocks from you. We'll drop you off, as long as you don't mind getting bashed about a bit in the back seat of my old blue slob," Jeremy said, using his Saab's nickname.

By the time Jeremy turned down Hill Street, and pulled up in front of the Preston house, Jonathan was in high spirits.

Jeremy got out of the small two-door car to let Jonathan unfold his long legs from the back seat.

"Thanks for the lift." Jonathan grinned, giving Jeremy's shoulder a friendly squeeze. "And nice meeting you, Di," he said, poking his head back into the idling car.

31

"Hey, Jonathan, wait up," Jeremy called out abruptly as Jonathan started down the winding gravel path to his house.

Jonathan walked back to the car and stuffed his hands in his pockets. The sky had cleared but the wind was up, and there was definitely a feeling of winter in the air. Jonathan's breath came out frosty, as he asked, "What's up? Did I forget something?" He peered through the dusty back window, then felt for the knapsack on his back. It was there.

Jeremy looked at Jonathan, half silhouetted by a street light. He tried to sound casual as he asked, "Are you free this Saturday afternoon?"

Jonathan thought a minute. "Until about six. Yeah, I am. Why? What's up?" He leaned back against the white picket fence enclosing the Prestons' front yard.

Jeremy dug in his pocket and pulled out a rumpled envelope. "I've got two tickets for the Army/Navy game at Annapolis."

Jonathan looked impressed and waited for Jeremy to continue.

"It turns out Di and I can't make it."

"What?" Diana gulped. "Jeremy — " she started to protest. Then suddenly her eyes widened in comprehension. "Oh, no," she muttered to herself and sank down in her seat. She didn't want to hear what Jeremy said next.

"Wow, that's tough. You should have no trouble getting rid of the tickets, though. *Everyone* I know wants to go to that game."

"Uh — not exactly," Jeremy interrupted quickly. He nervously tugged at his shirt collar, and swallowed hard. "You see," he improvised awkwardly, "My sister, Fiona she just got here more or less. She didn't expect to move with us to America, and she's having a rough time of it. Fiona doesn't know many people yet and she needs to get out. Actually, she'd love to do something typically American, like go to a football game. Especially an Army/Navy game. I was wondering if you'd like to go with her."

"What, me?" Jonathan sounded incredulous. "Go to an Army/Navy game?" He frowned slightly in the dark. "I mean it's real nice of you to ask, but — "

"No, listen," Jeremy insisted. "I'd really appreciate it if you could go." He tapped the envelope and said confidentially, "When I nabbed these I tried to get another ticket for Fiona, but they are — what's the expression? — as hard to find as a haystack."

Diana cracked up. "Jeremy, you mean 'as a needle in a haystack'." She secretly hoped Jeremy wouldn't be able to talk Jonathan into this blind date. It sounded all wrong to her. Picturing Fiona at a football game didn't seem right, either.

Jeremy plowed on. "You see," he said, lowering his voice and pacing back and forth in front of the car, "you'd be doing me a favor. Fiona really needs something to lift her spirits. You know she's a dancer. She's delicate, artistic, and sensitive. Not making it into the National Ballet when she's had her heart set on it since she was just a little kid has really messed her up. Fiona needs to get her mind off the dance world. She's got to expand her horizons. I guess you could say she's been kind of sheltered. Know what I mean?" Jeremy halted in front of Jonathan and looked at him expectantly.

Jonathan nodded slowly. "Sure. I mean why not? Football's not exactly my cup of — " He stopped himself before he sounded too ungrateful. "Actually, it's generous of you to offer the tickets, and I'd be glad to take your sister. It sounds like she *has* had a rough time." He shoved his hat back on his head and stared a minute at his feet. When he looked up he was grinning broadly. "Actually, Stone, what better way to get the feel of the good old U.S.A. in the fall than checking out a classic football game."

Jeremy grinned at the growing enthusiasm in his friend's voice. Jonathan was sounding like himself again. Maybe meeting Fiona would cheer Jonathan up, too. He congratulated himself on interesting Jonathan in Fiona before too many other girls realized the popular junior was available. Jeremy had no doubt in his mind Jonathan would really fall for his sister the minute he laid his eyes on her. He beamed as he passed the envelope into Jonathan's hands. Before Jonathan might have a chance to change his mind, Jeremy jumped back into the car and slammed the door. "I'll tell Fiona. And thanks, Jonathan. You'll like her."

"If she's your sister, I'm sure I will," Jonathan

said amiably, stuffing the tickets into his jacket pocket. He pushed open the white wooden gate, then turned around and yelled after Jeremy's car. "Tell Fiona I'll call her tomorrow after school — about when to pick her up and all."

But Jeremy's taillights had already vanished around the corner.

# Chapter
# *4*

"You know what my old dance teacher told us once?" Fiona said to Dierdre Patterson the next day. Like most of the Kennedy student body, the two girls had taken advantage of the clear, crisp autumn weather to spend lunch period on the quad.

"What?" Dee asked, leaning forward slightly. Fiona's stories of life at an English ballet boarding school intrigued her immensely.

"She said that whether or not a girl or boy went on from Kingsmont to become a professional dancer, the rigors of a dancer's life would teach them discipline and how to succeed at anything they put their minds to."

"She was right. I'm sure of it," Dee said firmly. "Any other kid moving here a couple of months into the semester would be struggling with so much school work. You're doing great, Fiona. I bet you make the honor roll."

"Do you think so?" Fiona asked, a little too quickly. Dee nodded. Fiona smiled and went on. "Jeremy said the same thing last night. But he tends to think I can do no wrong." Fiona felt funny mentioning Jeremy and their talk the night before. Her dismal mood seemed to have passed with yesterday's storm. But she still felt raw and shaky inside. She wasn't quite sure confiding in her friend was the best idea.

Fiona thoughtfully crunched on her apple, then revealed her plan. "You see Dee, I want to do well in school. I never thought about school work much before — I didn't have to." Fiona was amazed that she was able to keep her voice steady. "But now I've been thinking about what I want to do, if — if I'm not going to dance."

Dee started to interrupt.

Fiona didn't give her a chance. "Last night I thought maybe I might make a good doctor or physical therapist. I could help people with dance and sports injuries." Fiona paused, and searched her friend's open face. "What do you think?"

Dee pushed her silky ash blonde hair out of her face and looked directly at Fiona. "I think it's a great idea, Fiona. You'd have firsthand experience understanding dancers' problems." Her eyes sparkled with enthusiasm. "In fact, you should talk to Holly Daniels. Do you know her?"

"Sure. She's Bart Einerson's girl friend." Fiona suddenly felt uncomfortable. She didn't exactly want to talk to anyone but Dee about this yet.

37

"Well, Holly's planning to go to medical school."

"I don't think I'm ready to tell anyone else about this just now. I haven't even told my parents yet. I just wanted to get your reaction," she said, suddenly wishing she hadn't told Dee at all. Now she felt committed to something she wasn't ready for.

The bell rang out across the campus. Dee wrapped up her last stalk of celery and asked, "You going to dancercise today?"

Fiona shook her head. For the past few weeks Fiona had stood Dee up at the weekly workout. The last couple of times Fiona had walked into the dance studio, she'd felt slightly depressed.

"I can't go, either," Dee said wistfully. "Sasha asked me to cover the tryouts for *Oklahoma!* I like taking pictures more than sweating, but photographing dancers doesn't burn very many calories. I still have a couple of pounds to lose before Christmas."

"Trying to get to class on time after lunch burns up a few, though." Fiona quickened her pace across the quad. "And so does walking, by the way. How about walking home with me twice a week?"

"All the way home?" Dee squeaked. "That's about a zillion miles."

"Four miles to my house, and only three to yours. We can do it until the weather gets bad."

"I think I prefer dancercise, school buses, and rides with Marc," Dee said.

"We'll plan our walks the days Marc stays late

for practice." Fiona wasn't about to be put off.

"I'll make a deal with you," Dee returned, as they hurried down the hall. "You come to dancercise once a week; I'll walk with you twice a week. Unless it rains, snows, or hails."

Fiona swallowed hard. Going to a dance studio was going to be torture. Still, if she was going to deal with leading a totally new and different kind of life, she couldn't keep running away from everything that reminded her of the old one. "Okay, it's a deal. I'm walking home today, but you don't have to start until Monday."

"Tuesday — if it isn't snowing!" Dee corrected. "Don't forget dancercise Monday afternoon," she shouted behind her, making a beeline for her geometry class as the tardy bell rang.

At three o'clock Fiona stood in front of her open locker debating whether or not to change into her sneakers for the long walk home. She stared at the white running shoes lying on top of her crumpled gymsuit and was oblivious to the commotion in the crowded hallway. Sunlight poured through the glass brick windows and into her locker, decorated with a mini-poster of Baryshnikov. Fiona looked down at her feet and decided the sunshine was a good omen. She opted not to change out of her Italian loafers. She tossed some books into the locker and slammed it shut.

"Where *do* you get your shoes, Fiona?" Laurie Bennington cooed, suddenly appearing next to Fiona and walking beside her toward the exit.

"My trunk finally came," Fiona explained.

"I've been living out of a couple of suitcases until today. I love shoes," she added hastily.

"Hi Fiona, Laurie," Monica joined them after gathering her books and closing her locker. Kim Barrie was at her side.

"Where are those going?" Laurie eyed the sheaf of brightly colored posters spilling out of Kim's arms.

"Woody asked me to canvass the stores downtown to sell more *Oklahoma!* tickets and at the same time plaster Rose Hill with these posters for the show. He's busy with the tryouts. Everything's getting so frantic around here. I can't believe he has to have the show together in only a couple of weeks." Kim groaned. "I can't wait until it's over. Woody is driving me nuts."

Laurie frowned. "How does Woody get so many people to sell his tickets?" she grumbled. "I'm trying to sell ads for the yearbook, and I can't find enough staff to help. It seems like half the school's helping him out."

"Maybe you should bring it up at the student council meeting. Chris may have some suggestions. She's great at fund raising," Monica said.

"That is *exactly* what I intended to do," Laurie said as she marched out the door.

Monica giggled. "Poor Laurie. She keeps thinking Woody is waging some kind of war against her — and the yearbook!"

"Oh boy, I've got to run," Kim said, glancing up at the clock. "I borrowed the Earthly Delights van for the afternoon, and sparks are going to fly if I don't get it home exactly at five: Fifteen chicken pot pies have to be delivered to the D.A.R. meeting tonight in Maryville!"

Monica helped Kim gather up her posters, and said to Fiona, "Want a ride home? Peter and I are heading into D.C. to pick up some promo albums WRRK is donating to WKND. We'll pass pretty close to your house."

"I can't," Fiona said. "I — I have other plans." She suddenly felt stupid saying she didn't want a lift because she was going to walk home.

Monica arched her eyebrows. "Are you going to — "

"Monica!" Kim wailed from down the hall. "I'm never going to make it."

"Talk to you later," Monica said hurriedly, then bolted out the door after Kim.

Fiona started down the deserted hallway toward the side door. Maybe Jeremy was right. She should get more involved in school activities. Walking home alone didn't seem at all as appealing as walking with Dee. Watching the other girls head off to their various after-school projects suddenly made Fiona feel lonely and left out.

As she turned the corner, a familiar tune floated out of the open gymnasium doors. Fiona stopped in her tracks and cocked her head. She *almost* knew the words to the song. She hummed along for a second, totally off key. Then she frowned. Piano music in the gym at three o'clock on a Friday? Maybe the gymnastics team was practicing for a meet. A couple of the really good

41

gymnasts on the girl's team were in her PE section. She loved watching them. Fiona tiptoed to the door and peeked in.

Michael Rifkin was at the piano and Phoebe was next to him, straddling the piano bench, her cheek against his shoulder. Bart Einerson was leaning against the crook in the piano, a cowboy hat shoved back on his head and a guitar in his arms. When Fiona spotted Dee in the bleachers snapping pictures of a redheaded older woman talking to Woody Webster, she finally realized she had walked in on the dance auditions for *Oklahoma!*

Fiona was about to steal away when the woman clapped her hands. "Okay, let's try you boys." She motioned to a knot of guys standing awkwardly off to one side. They certainly didn't look like dancers; they looked like jocks. They were dressed in sweats and sneakers and Fiona recognized a couple of them as Marc Harrison's friends from the soccer team. "Michael," the woman said. "How about the intro to 'Kansas City'? Not too fast now."

The boys didn't budge from beneath the home team scoreboard.

"Come on, guys. Where's your school spirit?" Woody roared, moving across the floor in a couple of long-legged strides. He cornered a tall, well-built black guy who had on a varsity basketball sweater. "Gary, come on," Woody urged. "All of you. Line up — just do what Ms. Everson does. Try it, you'll *like* it."

The guys reluctantly lined up. Fiona stifled a

giggle. She suddenly pitied the drama teacher. These very unwilling stray athletes looked like pretty feeble substitutes for dancers.

Michael started to play and Ms. Everson demonstrated a very simple one-two-three-kick chorus line routine. It looked good, was easy, and went perfectly with the upbeat music. She motioned for Michael to stop playing.

"Your turn, boys." But when they started dancing, half kicked with their right foot, half with the left. Two of them headed to the right, the rest to the left. Not one of them moved in time to the music. Even worse, they looked scared to death and moved like stick figures. Fiona was sure she had seen some of these guys break dancing at Sasha's Halloween party. They probably *could* dance if they weren't so embarrassed, she thought. She sank against the doorway and covered her eyes.

"Unbelievable!" Woody suddenly yelled. Fiona hazarded a glance across the gym. "You guys are unbelievable." Woody pushed the straggly chorus line aside, and Michael stopped playing accompaniment. Phoebe stifled a giggle.

"Take it from the top, Mike." Woody grabbed Bart's cowboy hat, and plopped it at a crazy angle on his own head. Then he counted out a much faster rhythm for the same tune. He listened intently for a couple of bars, then broke into a long-limbed, goofy soft shoe routine. It was silly, but very good.

When Woody ended his zany routine, everyone burst into cheers and applause. "That's all folks!"

Woody "The Woodpecker" ad libbed as he shuffled "off-stage."

Fiona cracked up. Her high-pitched giggle carried across the gym and Woody looked up. Phoebe spun around to greet Fiona with a welcoming smile. "You did decide to try out — I'm *so* glad." Phoebe jumped up and started across the room.

Woody beat her. He arrived at Fiona's side, pulling Ms. Everson by the hand. "This, Ms. Everson, is a *real* dancer." As Woody explained Fiona's background, Ms. Everson noted her slender dancer's build, the slight turn-out of her legs, her long graceful neck, and perfect posture.

"Welcome to the Kennedy Players, Fiona. We could use your help." Ms. Everson arched her eyebrows and groaned under her breath, "You have no idea how much we need you."

Fiona's mouth fell open, her chin jutted forward. "Me!" She practically squeaked. "Sorry, there's been a mistake. I didn't — "

Woody grabbed Fiona's arm. "You see, we need someone not just to dance, but to choreograph the whole show. You'd practically be co-director with me. *Oklahoma!* is half ballet. And we can't find a single male dancer."

"But I didn't come here to try out," Fiona finally managed. Woody was practically dragging her across the floor to the improvised stage marked off with shiny silver tape.

Woody didn't listen. Ms. Everson broke in. "I understand. I can tell you'd be perfectly fine without an audition." Again she lowered her voice to

44

a whisper. "But it wouldn't be fair to the other girls, you know. If one person auditions, everyone has to."

Fiona fought back the rising sense of panic. Her head was spinning. She turned frantically to the bleachers, toward Dee.

Dee was on her feet focusing the zoom lens on her camera. She snapped a couple of shots of Fiona, then let the camera drop back around her neck. She flashed Fiona a victory sign, and mouthed "Good luck!"

"I can't. I just can't," Fiona gasped. "I'm not prepared. I haven't danced in weeks." No one was listening. Ms. Everson pointed Fiona towards a screened-off girls' changing area, then went back over to Michael. "Now boys, why don't you sit down for a while. Girls, let's line up and show these fellows what dancing's all about."

# *Chapter*
# 5

The dozen or so girls giggled and shoved and finally arranged themselves in two rows of a chorus line. Fiona lingered on the side line and pressed her fingers hard against her temples. Her head was pounding. "This can't be happening," she muttered to herself. Any minute she would wake up: The bubbly redheaded Ms. Everson, the gym, the tryouts would all be part of the same bad dream.

A second later, Michael began playing a lilting melody. Fiona closed her eyes. This was not a bad dream. The floor was not going to cooperate and open up and swallow her. Fiona couldn't just go running out of the gym, not in front of half of Jeremy's friends. She could sense Dee watching her from the bleachers, silently cheering her on. Her heart was racing and she could hardly catch her breath. She broke out in a cold sweat. But stage fright was nothing new to Fiona, and being scared triggered her into action. A part of her that had been numb and dead for weeks suddenly snapped to attention. All her highly trained dancer's instincts came to life. If she had to dance, she had to warm up or she'd get hurt. Her muscles were cold, stiff, and lazy from weeks away from dance class. She used the back of a nearby chair as a barre and did a couple of quick *pliés*, then kicked her legs front and back in loose swinging *battements*.

Ms. Everson finished giving some instructions to the girls, then stood in front of the line and motioned for Michael to continue playing. Fiona stripped off her sweater, and adjusted the straps of her leotard. She ducked behind the tallest girl she could find in the second row of dancers.

The drama coach demonstrated the first combination. Fiona craned her neck to see. It was an easy grouping of steps, right out of a beginning ballet class. When the music started up again, Ms. Everson stepped back to watch. Most of the girls were able to follow the steps. Fiona frowned with concentration as she danced. The steps were a cinch, but her style was wrong. She couldn't check herself in the mirror as she moved, but she could feel it. Her arms were too rigid and formal, her back too straight, and she hadn't kicked exactly like the teacher.

"Good," Ms. Everson said, and worked out a second, more difficult routine. As the girls tried to follow the steps this time, a couple dropped out.

Fiona went on dancing right to the end of the sequence, her face lighting up with a smile as she finished the final turn perfectly. I did better that time, she thought.

The teacher saved the trickiest dance for last. It was filled with subtle shifts in rhythm, hand claps, and lots of intricate head, shoulder, and hip movements. Michael played another familiar, fast-paced tune. Fiona didn't even notice how difficult the steps were, or how one by one all the other dancers gave up. This tune suited her dance style perfectly. A joyous smile spread on her face as she spun through the turns, hands on her slim hips. The music ended, and Fiona was still beaming as she held her closing pose a long silent second. The applause broke out around the gym and snapped her back to reality: She had just auditioned for a show, and from the look on Ms. Everson's face, Fiona knew she had gotten the job.

"Fiona, that was wonderful," Ms. Everson said over the general din that followed Fiona's performance. "Absolutely wonderful."

Woody jogged over to Fiona. He bent down and scooped up the petite dancer in his arms and swung her around and around, until Fiona shrieked with laughter. "Put me down. Oh Woody, please put me down."

"Nope!" Woody held her aloft. "Not until you promise to dance in our show, and choreograph it, and help with the production. I won't put you down unless you swear to be dance director of the whole deal!"

Fiona stopped squirming and the blush faded from her cheeks. She closed her eyes and considered the situation. How could she take on such a task? Dance in a show, choreograph a style she didn't understand at all, and help direct a bunch of kids she didn't know who weren't dancers. It seemed impossible — the whole project was doomed. Fiona was sure she couldn't face failing at something again.

Woody gave her a little shake. "Hey, up there. You're light as a feather, but I can't hold on forever. I'm no TV wrestler. Come on lady, stop playing hard to get. Can't you see how much we want you? We need you. Give in . . . before my shoulders do." Woody pretended to stumble.

Fiona wanted to say no, but some voice from deep inside her squeezed out yes. "Okay," she said, "I'll do it — I promise." Somehow she had to help make this show work. It would be an incredible challenge, but one that might help her feel more a part of things at Kennedy. She suddenly felt determined to come out of the slump she'd been in all these weeks, and she was elated. "Woody, I promised," Fiona cried out. "Now put me down."

"Everybody hear that?" Woody yelled to the cast.

A chorus of cheers greeted Woody as he lowered Fiona to the floor. Ms. Everson raised one hand to quiet the noisy room. "Rehearsals will resume Monday. The schedule will be posted outside the student activities room, so don't forget to check it first thing in the morning. We've only got a few more weeks before the play, and we haven't even begun the dance routines yet." She turned to Fiona and took her aside.

"I'm going to ask the students who tried out today to come back Monday. I'm afraid choreography for the boys is going to be very difficult. They can't do much. But the girls will be okay."

Fiona immediately agreed. "The girls were great. They all have a sense of rhythm. It's just a matter of picking up the style." Someone handed Fiona her sweater, and she pulled it over her head. She stared down at her feet a minute, then looked up directly into Ms. Everson's eyes. "About style, Ms. Everson, I really don't know much about musicals. My background's in classical dance. I'm pleased you want me to help, but I'm not sure I can do this."

"Nonsense," Ms. Everson said, dismissing Fiona's fears. "Your background is perfect. Any kind of dancer benefits from years of ballet training. You know that. As for style — well, *Oklahoma!* was the first American musical in which the dancers were just as important as the leads. In fact, the style is very balletic. You just have to familiarize yourself with the score and the cuts we've made. We can make more changes to accommodate the dancers — "

"Or lack of them!" Woody groaned.

Fiona considered Ms. Everson's words. She had thought all Broadway shows were the same when it came to dance. Lots of leggy girls and guys kicking and shaking their way through lots of routines that looked like the exercises in her dancercise class. "Well, I promised I'd do it," Fiona said, looking in Woody's direction, "and I'll try to do my best." She corrected herself quickly, "I *will* do my best."

"Fiona, you were terrific!" Dee said, bouncing down the bleachers to congratulate her friend. "The show can't help but be great now that you're part of it. Let's go to the sub shop to celebrate," she suggested as Woody, Michael, and Phoebe walked up to them.

"Did I hear the words 'sub shop'?" Woody cocked a hand behind his ear, and wiggled his eyebrows Groucho Marx style into Dee's startled face. Dee giggled, but Fiona grew serious. "No, I can't. Not today. If I really take this on — "

"IF!" Woody roared. He reached for Fiona.

She backed away with a shriek. "When I make a promise, I keep it. And if I'm going to do this right, I have to get the record and listen to the music, then look at a score, and read about the play. I don't know the first thing about it, you know." Fiona paused and gnawed her lower lip thoughtfully. "On the way home, I'll rent the video."

"Told you she was one of us," Woody crowed.

Fiona looked helplessly toward Phoebe. "What is he talking about?"

Phoebe chuckled. "The video. The whole cast is going over to Monica's tonight to watch it on her VCR. Woody came up with the brilliant suggestion at lunch a couple of hours ago. Monica volunteered her basement — and Kim's going to provide refreshments. In other words, a work/

study/party." Phoebe stuffed her hands into the pockets of her purple painter's paints. "And needless to say, now that you're part of the cast — "

Fiona listened to Phoebe with mixed emotions. Watching the video tonight with the kids in the show would be perfect. They could really brainstorm about choreography, and how to solve the problem of the male dancers. She already had an idea or two, but she needed to hear the music, see the show, and understand the story before airing them. On the other hand, the whole idea of dancing again was so new to her, she wasn't sure she should spend the evening with a big group of people talking about it. She needed time alone to get used to the idea. But then she remembered how Jeremy had accused her of isolating herself. Well, now was the time to change.

"So what do you say, Fiona?," Michael asked. "I've got to get going now, but Phoebe and I can bring you to Monica's later."

"Well. . . ." Fiona almost declined. "Okay," she suddenly decided. "I'll go, and I could use a ride. It'll be good to see the movie with the rest of the kids in the show. We can work out ideas together," she said, her enthusiasm growing. "Yes, I'd like that very much."

"I have a hunch our problems are about to be solved!" Jonathan Preston announced to Chris and Brenda, as he shoved open the swinging metal doors of the school shop. The usually noisy room was quiet and deserted. Its long workbenches were clean and the hand tools that normally littered the shop hung in neat rows on the walls. Jonathan checked a clock above the table saw. The student council meeting had dragged on longer than usual. He shouted, "Hey, Jacobs, you still around?"

"In here!" a deep voice boomed from the supply closet.

Jonathan turned to Chris and grinned. "We lucked out."

A dark-haired figure emerged from the storage room and came toward them, his black workboots squeaking across the linoleum. "You're late, Preston!" Matt said, pulling a denim jacket off a hook and slipping it on over his workshirt. Then he noticed Chris and Brenda. "Chris Austin," he said, suddenly turning shy. "Uh — what brings you to the shop?" he mumbled, then noticed Brenda standing back a few feet, looking at Matt shyly.

Chris cleared her throat. "I guess we came to ask a favor," she said. And turning to Brenda she added, "This is my sister, Brenda. Bren, this is Matt Jacobs, president of the Fix-It Club."

"Hi," Brenda said, stretching out her hand.

"Brenda Austin?" Matt seemed to recognize the name. "Aren't you the one involved with Garfield House? I've heard great things about that place," he said earnestly.

"Garfield's actually why we're here." Brenda smiled into Matt's dark eyes. "Jonathan thought you could help us out with a little problem."

Jonathan gulped. "It's not exactly a *little*

problem. The Holiday Homeless Drive needs a home," he joked. Matt groaned and leaned back against the table, arms folded across his muscular chest. He listened carefully as Jonathan continued. "The school custodian said we've got to move the food and clothing donations out of the gym by the end of next week. Garfield's volunteered its basement for storage space."

"But it's got to be cleaned out first," Chris went on. "And we need to hammer together some bins and get stuff categorized."

"Then we've got to move the donations from here to there," Brenda interjected. "Transportation is another problem. Jonathan told us you fix cars, and you have a couple of pickup trucks."

Matt stared thoughtfully at his boots. He kicked at a pile of sawdust, then looked up, a slow smile growing on his serious face. "I can volunteer my club for the work. Building stuff's a cinch for the guys and girls I work with, and I'm sure we can round up enough vans and small trucks to make the move." Then his face turned serious again. "This sounds like a great project. Lots of kids around school like the idea of a homeless drive, but they aren't good at dancing or singing, or they haven't been involved with the play to raise money. . . . This would give them a chance to be a part of things."

"Oh, Matt, this'll be good," Brenda said, as the three of them got ready to leave. "It's so nice of you to offer to help. I was really worried about getting all the work done by the end of next week."

When Matt was almost out the door he asked, "Hey, Jonathan, need a ride home?"

"More than that!" Jonathan groaned. "I need my car fixed by tomorrow for that blind date I told you about."

Matt punched Jonathan on the shoulder. "Sure thing. I'll grab my tools from the shop. We'll head straight for your house and I'm sure we can get Big Pink on the road in time for the game tomorrow."

Chris checked her watch and said, "Jonathan, let's try to catch the custodian before he leaves for the day. He'll probably have a better weekend knowing we've solved the problem of our overcrowded gym. Brenda, wait for me in the parking lot by the flagpole. I'll only be a few minutes."

Brenda and Matt slowly walked across the empty quad, not saying a word. Brenda stole a glance at Matt. He seemed like a thoughtful, quiet person — and very serious. She jumped up onto the concrete base of the flagpole and sat there, staring out into the afternoon sun. Matt eyed the spot next to Brenda, then looked down at his shoes. She smiled and invited him to sit down next to her. Instead, he crouched at the side of the concrete base, and picked up a clump of dried cut grass, shredding it as he talked.

"I'd like to hear more about Garfield. I hear you're really active there." Matt looked up at Brenda, his eyes very intense. "I'm interested in hanging out around that place myself. I'd like to help with the rap groups, and get some of the kids in my club involved. That's one reason I volunteered the Fix-It's services." He shifted his gaze and looked across the parking lot into the distance. "I wasn't kidding about lots of people wanting to help with the Holiday Drive but thinking they didn't have anything to contribute. Lots of kids feel like that."

"Yeah, I know what you mean. I used to think the same thing. It seemed like only the smart, stylish kids were meant to do important things," Brenda said, remembering all too well how she felt when she first came to Kennedy and was wary of people like Chris and her friends. "But it's not really like that at all. Anyone can get involved in a cause like this. You don't have to be part of any special group."

"I know." Matt surprised her by agreeing. "But some kids don't see it that way. I found out that what I do best — fix cars — teaches me lots of things about people. You'd be surprised at the number of heart-to-hearts I've had with a few tough, mixed-up characters over a lube job in the school shop. That's why I want to know about Garfield. Maybe I could help there."

Brenda's dark eyes opened up. "Matt, that would be wonderful," she said, grabbing his arm. "Why don't you come with me next week when I go to my rap group. You can meet Tony Martinez, the head counselor there, and see how the place operates. He's always looking for kids who want to help out. And I know he'd want to thank you in person for helping to move all the clothes and food and stuff to Garfield House."

"I'd like that," Matt said, then noticed Chris and Jonathan strolling toward them. He and Brenda stood up, and the four of them headed for the parking lot.

# Chapter 6

Fiona dumped the pile of records, sheet music, and books on the Stones' front hall table and eyed them ruefully. Michael had just raided his mother's music room to find all this material on *Oklahoma!* for Fiona. She rubbed her sore arms and squirmed out of her black bomber jacket. Tomorrow, Phoebe was going to drop off the marked version of the Kennedy Players' score, and tonight Fiona was going to watch the video at Monica's. A wave of panic washed over her. What had Fiona gotten herself into? She felt overwhelmed, but for the first time in weeks, really excited, too. The prospect of a busy weekend working out dance steps pleased her immensely.

She stacked the records and books at the foot of the staircase, and started toward the enormous, high-ceilinged living room with the sheet music in her hand. She was halfway toward the grand piano when the phone rang.

"Jeremy!" she called. "The phone." On the third ring, she hurried to answer it. Jeremy's coat was on the rack, his books stacked on a bench near the door. He was probably in the darkroom.

"Hello!" she said.

"Fiona?" a male voice asked. "Is this Fiona Stone?"

"Yes," Fiona answered suspiciously. She didn't recognize the voice on the other end.

"Uh — my name's Jonathan, Jonathan Preston. I'm a friend of your brother's," he explained.

"Oh, Jeremy's friend. Yes, I think he mentioned doing some photography with you last week. I'm sorry, he can't come to the phone right now. He's in the darkroom. Do you want him to ring later?" she asked, and reached for a pencil to take down Jonathan's number.

"No," Jonathan said quickly. There was a long pause before he continued. "Actually, I called to talk to you."

"To me?" Fiona leaned back against the wall and twiddled the cord. "Is it about the show? Woody said he was going to tell some more guys to talk to me about the auditions. We're still having them Monday if you're interested."

"The show?" It was Jonathan's turn to sound confused. "Oh!" He suddenly burst out laughing. "You think I'm calling about trying out for *Oklahoma!*"

Fiona nodded but before she could say anything, Jonathan was chuckling heartily. He could barely get the next few words out. "I'd love to, but you wouldn't want me if I were the only guy at Kennedy High. I'm totally unmusical. I can't carry a tune, and I'm a lousy actor. I have at least two — no, let me see — three left feet!"

Fiona giggled. Jonathan had a warm, friendly voice, and a pleasant laugh. She found herself wondering what kind of looks would go with such a voice. She closed her eyes and tried to picture him. He was probably tall, but not too tall, and definitely very handsome. When she tuned back in to what Jonathan was saying, her eyes popped open.

". . . and I thought you might like to go to a football game. The Army/Navy game is tomorrow, and thanks to your generous brother, I've got tickets. I just was calling to find out what time to pick you up — and to introduce myself," Jonathan explained.

"An Army/Navy game? Tomorrow?" Fiona sputtered. "You mean Jeremy set up a date for me and he didn't tell me? Why, you and I haven't even met." Fiona knew she sounded as horrified as she felt.

There was an awkward silence on the other end of the phone. "He didn't tell you I'd be calling? Sounds like we've got our wires crossed," Jonathan finally said.

Fiona forced herself to take deep breaths as she tried to regain control of her feelings. There certainly were some crossed wires here, and she was going to uncross them fast. But how? She frantically searched for excuses. But she had no idea what Jeremy told this guy. Anything she said would sound like a lie. She couldn't even think of any way out of it so she said, "Well, there's obviously been some kind of mistake. Jeremy must have forgotten to tell me. And since you made the plans and all, I'll go. I mean — " Fiona forced herself to say, "I'll be happy to go."

"Okay, then," Jonathan said briskly, "I'll pick you up around noon. It's not a long drive to Annapolis."

The second he hung up, Fiona flew across the room, through the hall, into the kitchen, and down the basement stairs. She headed for the playroom that Jeremy had converted into a darkroom. A bright sign Diana had painted for Jeremy was dangling from the doorknob. It said: PHOTOGRAPHER AT WORK. DO NOT ENTER ON PAIN OF DEATH.

When she threw open the door she was still holding the music from *Oklahoma!* in one hand.

The room was pitch black except for the glow of the safety light and the glimmer of afternoon sunlight Fiona had just let in.

"*Fiona!*" Jeremy howled. "What are you doing?"

Fiona defiantly flicked on the overhead light. Jeremy deserved to have all his pictures ruined. One look at her red-cheeked face, and the angry protests died on his lips. "How could you, Jeremy? How could you?" Fiona ranted, waving the sheet music in her brother's astonished face. "Fixing me up like that. With some guy I've never

61

met, as if I were the last girl at Kennedy High desperate for a date. How could you?" Fiona repeated, her bottom lip beginning to tremble.

He put aside his darkroom tongs and shifted to face his sister. "Jonathan's a very nice guy. He wouldn't think that about you."

"*He* wouldn't. Well what about you? I've never been so insulted in all my life. I want an apology, Jeremy."

Jeremy looked down and swirled a ruined print around in the developing tray. "What did you say to him? You didn't yell at him, Fiona, did you?" Jeremy looked at her, his face full of concern for Jonathan.

"What could I possibly have done, on the spot like that? I certainly had had no warning, and I couldn't think of an excuse, so I told him I'd go." Jeremy closed his eyes and heaved a deep sigh of relief as Fiona continued her tirade. "But you could have asked me first. I don't have time for football games and nonsense like this."

Jeremy shook his head. "Fiona, that's not true. You've been — "

"Whatever I've been doing, I'm not doing it anymore," Fiona interrupted. "I'm going to be very busy now. I'm the dance director of *Oklahoma!* and starting tonight, I have to eat, breathe, and sleep the music if I'm to get that crazy crew of dancers into any shape to perform in a couple of weeks."

"Dance director?" Jeremy stared at his sister. His blue-gray eyes lit up. "So you auditioned after all." He threw his head back and laughed.

"Fiona, I knew you could do it."

Fiona gave a disgusted little shake of her head, but her blue eyes sparkled with pleasure at Jeremy's enthusiasm. For a second she almost forgot she was angry. "Jeremy, you must promise me one thing."

Jeremy tried to look solemn. "Whatever you wish, dear sister."

"Never, ever set up a date for me again. If you do I'll — I'll — "

"Kill me," Jeremy supplied helpfully, knowing that once Jonathan and Fiona met, he'd never *have* to set up a date for her again.

"No. I'll lurk outside this darkroom and turn on the lights and ruin every roll of film you expose. I swear I will, so you'd better promise." Jeremy had a hunch Fiona didn't make idle threats.

"Okay, okay. I promise!" He tried to seem apologetic, but he couldn't keep the smug look of satisfaction off his face. So far his plan for Fiona and Jonathan was working — not smoothly — but nevertheless, it was working. And he couldn't resist adding, "But you know I won't have to. I know you'll have a great time with this guy."

Fiona rolled her eyes. She leaned back against the counter and stared at her brother in disbelief. "And what makes you so sure of that?"

Fiona's sarcasm went right over Jeremy's head. "For starters, Jonathan's a real motivator around Kennedy."

"Most of your friends are," Fiona said.

Jeremy went on. "He's just been named the new student activities director."

Fiona groaned. "The rah-rah type. Just what I've always dreamed of." She gave a bored sigh.

"He comes from this really crazy family. When I went to his house, I thought I had walked into the set of one of those American sit-coms you see on the TV."

"My blind date," Fiona winced. "A guy straight out of 'Happy Days.' "

"I knew it!" Jeremy jumped up. "I knew he'd be perfect." He didn't seem to notice the despairing look on his sister's face. "Wait till you hear this. He's got this really wild pink '57 Chevy convertible. He fixed it up himself," Jeremy concluded proudly. "Back home, no one I knew fixed cars."

"Certainly no one I hoped to know, either," Fiona mumbled. "And what does this typical American guy look like?" she asked. She stopped kicking her foot against the shelf and held her breath a second, waiting for Jeremy's answer.

Jeremy considered Fiona's question carefully. He sensed girls would find Jonathan good looking, but he wanted to be sure Fiona got the message this guy wasn't just somebody looking for a date. "I can't say exactly, maybe a little like Robert Redford and Harrison Ford combined."

"Sounds like your generic Hollywood movie star," Fiona snapped. "Doesn't sound like my type at all," she added, marching straight out of the darkroom.

Jeremy's mouth dropped open.

"By the way, you can get your own dinner tonight. Mom and Dad are at a banquet, and I have plans later this evening. It turns out I'm capable of finding my own parties to go to," Fiona yelled back over her shoulder. "And besides, I've just lost my appetite."

A few hours later Fiona sat on the floor of Monica Ford's family room, doing some of her dancing stretches, and waiting for Monica to turn on the video. Janie Barstow sat cross-legged beside her and took notes, as her boyfriend Henry Braverman talked to Fiona about the problems of designing costumes for the dancers.

"You'll need to use gussets!" Fiona practically shouted into Henry's ear. The noise in the room was unbearable. Fiona could barely hear the original cast album of the show blasting from the stereo. At least talking shop to Henry kept her mind off her fight with Jeremy and the dismal thought of spending a Saturday afternoon with a guy who she didn't even know.

"Gussets?" Janie repeated, her soft voice cracking as she struggled to make herself heard.

Fiona nodded vigorously. "Yes, under the arms. And lots of stretchy fabric wherever there's stress. Like around the waist."

"And good fabric, too," Henry commented. "I sat in on a costume designing workshop at the Regional Theatre in Maryville recently. They said you need good fabrics to hold up under the harsh stage lights."

"Uh-huh, and it's more important for dance

costumes. You're moving so fast, the audience needs to have a strong visual impression. Real velvet, for example always looks better than velveteen. You need durable, first-quality stuff, because they need to be cleaned more often. Because of the sweat."

Janie's golden eyes grew wide. Fiona looked so delicate, like something out of a fairytale. Janie couldn't picture her sweating.

"You also have to lightly hand sew all the sequins and trim. Or else they — "

Henry put up his hand and stopped Fiona. "I can't hear a thing you're saying." The noise level had just gone up several decibels. Woody and Bart were clowning around over by the sofa in their cowboy hats.

"Hey, will the rodeo contingent please pipe down!" Henry yelled in a surprisingly booming voice. The tall, slender designer was usually soft-spoken. "Some of us are trying to get work done. Remember, this is a working party!" Henry reminded them good-naturedly.

Fiona frowned slightly as she watched Woody and Bart pretend to have a shoot-out with their fingers. She got a feeling Woody wasn't quite serious enough to pull the production together.

Monica yelled from the corner where she was manning the popcorn popper. "Henry's right. Peter, let's put on the video now. And really, folks, I am looking forward to seeing it — and *hearing* it."

A second later, Peter dimmed the overhead lights, and the noise died down.

Fiona tucked her legs under her and focused her attention on the screen. The opening sequence was very beautiful: A cowboy riding a horse through the beautiful Oklahoma countryside. As he sang "Oh, What a Beautiful Morning," the credits rolled down the screen. Fiona leaned forward into the light bouncing off the TV set. When she saw the name of the choreographer, she gasped "Agnes DeMille!"

Woody's voice was suddenly behind her. He crouched down and said, "She's one of the real greats, isn't she? I wasn't sure she was famous over in England."

"Famous?" Fiona whirled around and eyed Woody. "She's one of the greatest choreographers of the century. What she did for dance!" Fiona sighed. DeMille was one of her heroines.

Woody went on. "What I like is the way she combined all those folk styles. The down-home dancing with real ballet."

"I didn't know you knew about dance," Fiona said, surprised.

Phoebe trotted up with a bowlful of popcorn. "That's show biz," she said, snapping Woody's suspenders. "And when it comes to show biz, Woody's the pro around here."

"In the acting and music department — not in the dance department," Woody corrected, shoveling a handful of popcorn into his mouth. He passed the bowl to Fiona. She picked out a couple of plump kernels, and passed the bowl down the line to Janie and Henry.

"Well, I don't know that I'm a pro at this stuff,"

Fiona admitted. "I don't know the first thing about square dancing."

"It's pretty easy to learn," Woody encouraged. "Today at the audition you picked up the right style just watching Ms. Everson go through the steps once. I must have watched her ten times and the message never quite got down to my feet."

"Well, I've been trained to catch on quickly to new sequences of steps," Fiona said. "But how am I going to learn all these American Western dances?"

"Hey, I have a great idea!" Woody shouted. "There's a country music club in Maryville. It's called 'The Barn Dance.' They get some of the best folk and square dance bands to play there. If you go there some night and check them out, you'll be drowning in inspiration."

"Sounds perfect!" Fiona's face lit up. "When are the dance nights?" she asked, her pencil held to her notebook.

"Tomorrow's one — that's Saturday, starting some time in the afternoon. And Wednesday evenings, too, I think."

Fiona's face fell. Of all the rotten luck. Tomorrow she was stuck going to a football game with Jonathan. If she didn't have this crummy date, she could get Dee and Marc to go out with her.

"Hi, everybody. Did we miss the movie?" Marc Harrison bounced down the dozen steps leading into the finished basement and greeted the crowd.

Dee poked her head out from under his arm, and waved at Fiona. Fiona was glad to see Dee.

She had to talk to someone about Jonathan and this crazy date, even if it was too late to get out of it.

"What's up?" Dee asked, joining Fiona in front of the TV. Peter had turned on the lights again, and Fiona had given up trying to watch the movie. There was too much noise to concentrate on the music and the story. She tried to force back a rising sense of annoyance. This party was exactly that: a party. No one seemed remotely interested in brainstorming on the production.

"Plenty!" Fiona began to confide. She quickly cut herself off when Ted Mason and Marc sauntered over. Soon she found herself in the middle of a conversation about the next day's Army/Navy game.

Dee flashed Fiona a puzzled look. "I can't believe you even *know* about the game."

"I'm going," Fiona said flatly. She looked up quickly at the guys, but they didn't seem to have heard.

"You're *what*?" Dee cried. "How'd you get so lucky? Wait until I tell Marc — "

"No!" Fiona wailed, then dropped her voice. "I've got to talk to you." She pulled Dee over to the stairs. They sat down on the bottom step and began to talk.

After she told Dee about the phone call and Jeremy's setting up a blind date, Fiona looked helplessly at Dee and said, "What am I going to do? I don't want to go. It was all so embarrassing — I had to say yes. And now I can't go to that country music club and watch the dancing.

Monday I have to start choreographing the show, and I'm not at all prepared. I could really kill myself."

"Don't worry so much, Fiona. It's not worth it. We'll work something out about the club. As for your date, chances are you won't like each other. You'll go out this one time, realize you're not made for each other, and that'll be the end of it. It's just one afternoon." Dee stopped talking long enough to savor her allotment of one handful of popcorn. She crunched the last kernel then asked, "Did Jeremy say what this guy looks like?"

"A cross between Robert Redford and Harrison Ford, if you can believe that."

"What?" Dee gasped. She sank back against the stairs and pretended to faint. "You're going on a blind date with someone who looks like that? How did I miss a guy like that around the halls of Kennedy High?" Dee giggled, then lowered her voice. "Don't tell Marc I said that. *Please.*"

"My lips are sealed!"

"Of course, maybe Jeremy just made that up. He's a great photographer, but he doesn't exactly notice things," Dee observed.

"Tell me about it." Fiona shook her head in disgust. She tugged her stirrup pants over her socks and propped her chin on her knees.

"Did he mention his name?" Dee asked.

"Of course — Jonathan Preston."

"Jonathan Preston!" Dee shrieked, then looked around the room and dropped her voice to a whisper. "He doesn't look like Robert Redford or Harrison Ford. But he's one of the cutest guys at school, and everyone likes him. He's laid back, sort of easygoing."

Fiona didn't look convinced. Dee caught Phoebe's eye, and waved her over toward the steps.

"Phoebe, tell Fiona what Jonathan Preston is like," Dee urged.

"Dee!" Fiona cringed. She didn't want her blind date broadcast all over Monica's basement.

"Jonathan?" Phoebe's face opened into a sunny smile. "He's great. He's single-handedly done more for the school in the past couple of months than any other student activities director. He's a lot of fun, too."

"I told you, Fiona," Dee said gleefully, then pulled Phoebe down next to them on the bottom step. "Pheeb, Jonathan is taking Fiona to the Army/Navy game tomorrow. Jeremy set it all up. Isn't that great?"

Phoebe glanced at Fiona. She looked pretty depressed about the whole thing, but something about the idea of her and Jonathan together didn't seem so wrong. "Hey, cheer up," she said to Fiona. "Jonathan's a nice guy. Half the girls at Kennedy would give their right arm to go out with him."

Fiona sighed. No matter what Dee and Phoebe said, she was convinced that her date with Jonathan at the Army/Navy game was going to be one of the longest, dullest afternoons of her life.

# Chapter 7

Saturday started out cold and gray and Fiona hoped the game would be canceled. It was a perfect day to listen to records and block out dance steps in front of her mirror. If the football game was canceled she could phone Dee and they could go to The Barn Dance. When she suggested this at breakfast, Jeremy laughed. "Football is played in rain, snow, sleet, or hail."

All morning long, Fiona continued to hope that Jonathan wouldn't show up. But at the stroke of noon, the doorbell rang twice. Fiona grimaced at her reflection in the hall mirror, brushed a fleck of mascara off her cheek, and hurried down the hall. She paused with one hand on the doorknob and took a deep breath. She didn't want Jonathan to get the idea that she was the least bit nervous about this idiotic blind date. She promised herself, one last time, to be nice to Jeremy's friend

— no matter how boring and difficult the afternoon turned out to be.

She flung open the door and suddenly she forgot her carefully prepared introduction. Fiona found herself looking way up at a tall guy, straight into a pair of startlingly penetrating gray eyes. He didn't look the least bit like the Hollywood hero Jeremy had described. He looked more like the David Bowie poster Fiona had over her bed, even though he *was* wearing a soft Indiana Jones-style hat. The gray felt made his eyes seem even grayer.

As she watched him watch her, the expression in his eyes changed from friendly to surprised to something that made her spine tingle. She shivered and forced herself to look away.

"Uh, I'll get my jacket," she stumbled, and stepped back into the hall. Fiona grabbed her short denim jacket off the coatrack, and tugged it over her long sweater. Suddenly, she remembered she hadn't introduced herself. She didn't even know if this was Jonathan.

"I'm Fiona," she said, noticing for the first time his absolutely awful, moth-eaten raccoon coat. It looked like something her grandfather might have worn to a 1930s rugby game. It was positively disgusting.

He tilted his hat back and said with a nervous grin, "Oh, yes. I mean, I figured that."

He shifted his gaze away from her face and intently studied the porch railing, then his loafers. Finally he focused on a point over Fiona's right shoulder. She turned around nervously, wondering what he was looking at. He seemed to be studying the brass numbers tacked to the shingles.

"I'm Jonathan Preston," he said sticking out his hand. His voice *was* the same warm friendly voice she remembered from the phone. Fiona shook his hand. It was firm and dry and very pleasant to touch, but when the deep fur cuff on his sleeve brushed her wrist, she cringed. She suddenly didn't know if she was relieved or disappointed that the guy towering over her really was her blind date.

Jonathan, in turn, jammed his hands into his pockets, and started down the porch steps. "I'd like you to meet 'Big Pink,' " he mumbled.

"Who?" She hesitated at the foot of the steps. Jonathan was headed toward the biggest pink convertible Fiona had ever seen. "Oh no!" she groaned. She was sure she didn't like people who named their cars — though the name was certainly appropriate. It hogged at least three parking places along the curb, and had weird, winglike tail fins. The black canvas top was full of holes and the color was appalling. Fiona wondered if he had chosen the color himself. It was so dreadfully loud. She ran to catch up to him. When she got close, Jonathan fingered her jacket and looked her up and down. He didn't seem to like what he saw.

Fiona backed away. She had dressed so carefully that morning. She wanted to look very sharp, cool, but not overly interested. She just wanted to be sure he knew the instant he saw her that she was not some desperately shy outsider who needed to be fixed up on a blind date. She had settled on a black and green geometrically patterned sweater, a black miniskirt, tights, and her favorite ankle boots. She had been quite pleased with her reflection in the mirror last time she checked it.

"You're going to be cold," he said. "But as the Boy Scouts say: Be prepared!" He flung open the back door of the car and pointed to a raccoon coat that matched his.

"You can wear this," he said, yanking the coat out from under two red and yellow cheerleading pom-poms and a bull horn.

"*That*!" Fiona gasped. "Why, it looks like the fleas have been at it." As Jonathan offered the coat, she shrunk back disgustedly. Even if it weren't moth-eaten, she'd die before she'd wear such a corny outfit to a football game. "My jacket's just fine, thank you," she said curtly as she slid into the passenger seat. Fiona settled back on the torn upholstery, trying to keep her legs out of range of a protruding spring.

Jonathan misinterpreted Fiona's response. "Oh, I didn't mean it like that. Your jacket's great. It doesn't look very warm, though. I just found these up in the attic, and I thought they were hilarious. Warm, too." He held out the coat a second longer, then shrugged and tossed it back onto the seat. "It gets very cold in the stadium."

By halftime, Fiona was convinced she was dying of exposure. He calls this cold! Frigid's more more like it! she fumed inwardly. Army was leading the hometeam, Navy, by a score of 21–14. Fiona sat shivering on the icy metal bench half-

75

way up to the grandstands above the fifty yard line. She wasn't very fond of the idea of the military, and the stands were full of uniformed cadets and midshipmen who fit her picture of loud, boisterous American college men perfectly. She felt like she was witnessing a minor war and not a sport. Leave it to Jeremy's Yankee friend to take her on a date like this!

She craned her neck, looking for Jonathan. He had disappeared ages ago to get something warm to drink. She glanced at her watch. Where was he? Her toes were so numb she couldn't feel her feet as she stamped them on the concrete to regain some circulation.

To think she was enduring this torture when she could be dancing and working on the show. Doing something that mattered, instead of wasting her time at a ridiculous football game, with a guy who insisted on shouting and cheering, no matter what was going on down on the field. She clenched her teeth so they wouldn't chatter, then turned up the collar of her jacket and tugged down her miniskirt. She willed herself not to shiver or be miserable, but to look simply as bored as she truly felt. She had said she'd go on this date and Fiona was determined to suffer through the afternoon with style. Besides, she would not give Jonathan Preston the satisfaction of saying "I told you so." Fiona had made him leave that repulsive coat in the car. What a weird sense of humor he had.

"Here, this will warm you up." Jonathan was back from the concession stand, at last.

Fiona looked up. His eyes matched the dark gray sky now. She took a perverse pleasure in seeing that in spite of his precious coat, he didn't look very warm, either. He offered her a steamy styrofoam cup. His hand was chapped and the skin was rough as it grazed hers. A shot of warmth went up Fiona's spine.

She caught her breath, then squashed herself down into her jacket for warmth. Guys she didn't like weren't supposed to affect her this way. And she didn't like Jonathan, she was sure of that. He was nice enough, just like Dee and Phoebe had said. But he was too superficial, too silly, and too predictable. He hadn't talked about one meaningful thing all afternoon. Every time she mentioned dance, or England, or Kingsmont, he tried to change the subject. Obviously she bored him as much as he bored her. She had hoped he would at least be cool enough to poke fun at the game. He wasn't. He really was the rah-rah type. When the pep squad cheered, Jonathan cheered just as loudly. He jumped up and down, and tried to get Fiona to join in the frenzied commotion surrounding them. But she had no idea why she was supposed to get excited every time some poor guy was practically trampled to death down on the field.

"How long do we have to endure halftime?" she muttered, eyes fixed on the colorful marching band parading up and down the field.

"Not much longer." Jonathan's smile looked a bit forced. "The game'll start up again soon. The teams switch goal posts. *We* haven't lost yet."

Fiona groaned and sipped her drink. It was a

very plastic-tasting version of hot chocolate. "It figures. American fast food," she grumbled, but downed it anyway. It was hot and she had never been so cold in her life. Heaving a loud sigh, she tucked her empty container beneath the seat and stared drearily at the band as it filed off the field. "Are all football games so military?" she asked. Their seats were on the Navy side, right behind the pep squad. Fiona glanced down at the cheerleaders and said, smugly, "I don't know what they have to cheer about. Aren't these sailor chaps losing?" Her tone was mocking, slightly disdainful. Her light, high voice seemed to carry above the general din.

"Shhhsh, Fiona!" Jonathan flashed her a warning glance.

"What? Did I say something wrong?" Fiona asked offhandedly.

Before Jonathan could reply, a roar filled the stadium as the two teams once again took the field. The initial commotion had barely died down when the Navy quarterback faked a couple of passes then ran the ball down the field. Every spectator in the home team section jumped up — everyone except Fiona. The noise was deafening. Fiona covered her ears and sank down further in her seat. She didn't hear the chorus of catcalls just behind her. She only felt Jonathan yank her to her feet.

"I'm not in the mood to get into a fight. Get up!" he ordered in a harsh whisper.

Fiona stared at Jonathan blankly. He looked very annoyed. "What are you talking about?

What did I do now?" she asked, pulling out of his strong grip. Then a note of fear crept into her voice. "What's happening?" she gasped.

"Navy just tied the score. Our friends behind us think you aren't happy enough about it. You could at least *pretend* to be happy." Jonathan's voice was tense. He thought a second, then declared, "It might be better to get out of here now." After a pause he added, "I don't think either of us is having a very good time."

It was the first thing he said all day that Fiona could agree with. She pushed her way after Jonathan down the long row of fans. As they reached the aisle it began to drizzle. By the time they reached Jonathan's car, the drizzle had turned to sheets of icy rain. Fiona stood shivering by the car door while Jonathan fumbled with his keys.

"You'd better put that other coat on. You're soaked to the bone," he said.

"I'm not interested in wearing your ratty coat." It was suddenly a symbol. She would not pretend to like any of this American gung-ho stuff one minute longer. Through chattering teeth she stammered, "I just want to go home!"

Jonathan threw his hands up in the air, then slammed Fiona's door shut and ran around to his side of the car. He climbed in and faced Fiona squarely. His eyes were smoldering as he said, "What's your problem, anyway? You're cold and wet and miserable and you still refuse to put on the coat. It's not doing the seat any good. In fact, if it stays back there it's going to get wet." Fiona arched her eyebrows at what she thought was more of Jonathan's silliness. But this time he wasn't joking. "The roof leaks over the back seat."

Fiona turned around in horror. The rain was beginning to puddle on the seat near the coat. She looked up quickly. Right above her head the black convertible top looked pretty solid. "I thought you *fixed* cars," she muttered, making a big thing of shaking the water out of her hair.

Jonathan glared at her. "You know you're acting worse than Kate — "

"Who's Kate?" Fiona asked suspiciously.

"My six-year-old sister," Jonathan replied.

"Well, if you didn't treat me like a six-year-old, maybe I'd act differently!" Fiona declared, her voice rising.

"What are you talking about?" Jonathan shook his head in disgust. He slammed his fist against the steering wheel and glared at Fiona. "Jeremy said you'd never been to a football game and I thought you'd be interested in seeing one."

"You've got to be kidding," she said haughtily. "Going to this dumb game wasn't *my* idea."

"Well, it certainly wasn't *mine!*" Jonathan snapped.

Fiona gaped at Jonathan in disbelief. "Come off it. You're the one who invited me," she sputtered, then challenged snidely, "And if it wasn't your idea, whose was it?"

"Jeremy's, of course," Jonathan stated. "And I should never have let him talk me into this."

"What?" Fiona roared. She knew Jeremy had

set up this ridiculous date, but she couldn't believe he'd suggest Jonathan take her to a football game. She'd have preferred something more . . . well . . . cultural. "Jeremy asked *you* to take *me* to an Army/Navy game?"

"He sure did," Jonathan yanked his felt hat off and tossed it behind him. It landed in the puddle on the back seat. He finally turned on the ignition. "And I had much better things to do today."

"So did I," Fiona returned icily. She eagerly stretched her hands toward the heating vent. A blast of frigid air met her fingers. She held them there anyway. "I've got to get at least a rough idea of what to do with *Oklahoma!* by Monday. I don't even know where to begin. Woody told me about country dancing at a club called The Barn Dance. I could be there now!"

"So all you really wanted to do today was dance?" Jonathan was suddenly confused. Jeremy had told him Fiona never wanted to dance again.

"Is that such a crazy idea? I am a dancer," Fiona said testily.

Jonathan took a deep breath. Jeremy had told him to try to get Fiona interested in something other than dance. He had also told him Fiona loved the idea of football. Jonathan raked his fingers through his straight blond hair. "You might have made life easier for both of us today if you had told me you wanted to go dancing." His voice still had an edge to it. He was beginning to wonder if the sharp-tongued, stubborn girl across the seat from him in the car was really Fiona Stone. Jeremy had described his sister as a shy, sad, lonely girl.

After a long silence, Fiona snapped, "You know, if you'd put the heater on 'hot air' maybe it would warm up in here."

"The heater's broken," Jonathan explained.

Fiona stared daggers at him. A second later he grabbed the coat from the back seat, and thrust it toward Fiona. "Put this on, or I won't drive you home," he commanded, turning off the ignition.

"What right have you — " Fiona cried. But she was too tired and miserable to protest. Jonathan just sat there arms folded across his broad chest staring fiercely out the windshield at the rain. Even if the coat looked like moths had been at it, it did look warm.

Fiona shuddered, made a face, and reached for it.

Jonathan grabbed it first. He shook it out, and awkwardly dusted it off. He didn't say a word. His lips were drawn into a narrow line as he helped her put it on. But his rough hands were incredibly gentle. His fingers grazed the back of her neck and Fiona trembled. She looked up, and her eyes locked on his. For a second she felt herself irresistibly drawn to him.

She squeezed her eyes shut and pulled away. "Thank you," she murmured. Fiona looked out the window to hide the color rising in her cheeks. She clutched the coat tightly around her neck and pressed her forehead against the glass. It stung her burning face. She felt puzzled and confused over the effect Jonathan had on her. He meant nothing to her — he belonged to some girl who just liked to have fun, joke around, and hang out. They had nothing in common. He was certainly not the boy of her dreams.

They rode home in silence. When they pulled up in front of her house, Jonathan reached across her lap and managed not to touch her as he threw open her door. "See you around," he mumbled.

Fiona climbed out. Keeping her back to Jonathan, she tossed the coat into the car, and ran shivering up the wide porch steps. "Not if I can help it!" she muttered, fishing in her bag for her key.

But as she reached the heavy oak door, she turned around, and watched Jonathan pull away from the curb. When the car had turned the corner, she took a deep breath and rubbed her chapped hand against her cheek, then against the back of her neck where Jonathan had touched her.

His touch had felt like a soft gentle kiss. And the spot still felt alive, tingly, more awake than any other part of her body.

"What's happening to me?" she whispered. She blew on her hands trying to warm them, then put her key in the door. The whole date with Jonathan had gone even worse than she had expected. It was the most terrible experience of her life. She had hated it — every moment of it. But if that were the case, why did she have this funny, empty feeling in the pit of her stomach at the thought of never seeing him again? More confused than ever, Fiona entered the house and slammed the door shut behind her.

# *Chapter*
# *8*

$D$ee Patterson held the cream-colored angora sweater up to her face and anxiously studied the the effect in the clothing store's dressing room mirror.

"No," Fiona said firmly. "It matches your complexion a little *too* perfectly. I can't tell where you end and the sweater begins. Try this." She shoved a golden yellow v-neck into Dee's hands. Dee eyed it skeptically, but obediently pulled it over her head. In matters of dress and makeup, Fiona had become Dee's personal fashion consultant. Her daring sense of color and dramatic combinations of accessories made her one of the most stylish girls on the Kennedy campus. That was one reason Dee had begged her to go on a Saturday night shopping spree to celebrate reaching her goal: it was several weeks before Christmas and Dee had finally lost her thirty-fifth and last pound. The other reason was to hear all about Fiona's blind date.

Dee's eyes shone with satisfaction as she stared at her reflection. The sweater seemed to bring out the golden highlights in her hair and eyes, and make her skin look incredibly creamy. It also showed off her still curvy, but now slim, figure. "Fiona, you really do have a knack with clothes," she remarked. "I'm glad you came with me tonight. Reaching the end of a diet isn't exactly something to celebrate with your boyfriend."

Fiona was enjoying the rare Saturday evening outing with Dee. Since her friend had started dating Marc, Fiona had been spending most Saturday nights alone. But tonight Marc had gone to Williamsburg on a field trip. Fiona really hadn't wanted to spend the night alone after her miserable afternoon with Jonathan, and when Dee called, she had jumped at the chance to get out of the house.

A little while later, the two girls were settled at one of the white metal tables at Tossed Salad, a new restaurant on the balcony of Rose Hill Mall's airy atrium.

"So tell me," Dee asked, carefully pouring dressing on her chef's salad, "how did it go with Jonathan? And who won the game?"

Fiona stared at her plate. She poked her fork into a limp bit of spinach, and sighed. "I don't know who won the game."

Dee's eyes widened. "How'd you manage to miss the score?"

"We didn't stay till the end," Fiona said softly. She began tearing the green border off her napkin.

"Oh." Dee sounded disappointed, but she figured there must have been a good reason for leaving early. Fiona looked even prettier than usual tonight: her blue eyes had a faraway dreamy look in them. Her cheeks were flushed. She had a sad, slightly mysterious air about her. Dee had a feeling Fiona was in love. She wondered if Jonathan had kissed her. "Where'd you go then?" she asked casually. Dee leaned forward in her seat, anxiously awaiting Fiona's answer.

"Home. I made him take me home," Fiona said tensely, then looked up from her plate. Bits of green and white paper littered the table in front of her. She hadn't eaten a bit of salad. "It was a disaster, an absolute disaster, Dee. We ended up fighting."

"You fought with Jonathan?" Dee was stunned. Jonathan had a reputation for getting along with just about everybody. "About what?"

"Everything, anything." Fiona began talking swiftly. She quickly reviewed the day's events. "It was such a waste of time," she concluded. "At least I got it over with and Jeremy promised he'd never, ever set up a date for me again."

"Will he have to?" Phoebe teased, as she and Holly Daniels walked up to the table in time to hear Fiona's last statement. "According to Jeremy, you and Jonathan are made for each other," she said, pulling over two chairs.

"What?" Fiona gasped. She fingered the

buttons on her baggy paisley shirt and stared down at her feet.

Phoebe was about to sit down. She bit her lip and gazed from Dee to Fiona to Holly. It was Holly who asked, "Is it okay if we join you? If you're having a heavy conversation, I mean we — "

Fiona motioned for Holly and Phoebe to sit down. "No, it's fine. We were just talking about the game this afternoon." Since everyone knew about her blind date already, everyone might as well hear about how badly it went, too.

"What are you two doing here on a Saturday night?" Dee asked, trying to change the subject.

"Michael's off in Georgetown looking at sound equipment with Peter." Phoebe propped her chin in her hands, and regarded Fiona with some curiosity. She sounded down, but looked great.

"And Bart's in Williamsburg, with Ted and Marc," Holly explained.

"So did Preston survive his first football game?" Phoebe asked Fiona, her green eyes twinkling with amusement.

"His what?" Fiona sat forward in her chair. "You mean he's never gone to a football game before?"

"He loathes them. He doesn't like the violence," Holly said. "But Phoebe's exaggerating. Today's game was his second this season. That's apparently some sort of record. He did go to the Leesburg game this year, the one where Bart got hurt. Matt Jacobs dragged him, saying no responsible student activities director should pass up a chance to cheer at the biggest game of the year."

"Well today he cheered with the loudest of them," Fiona snorted, then looked directly at Phoebe. "He didn't act like he hated it at all."

"Maybe he just liked the company," Holly quietly noted.

Fiona caught her breath and stared wide-eyed at Holly. Then she glanced quickly down at her plate. She felt her cheeks redden. Had Jonathan Preston actually *liked* her? No. Absolutely not — it was a crazy idea. He had told her she was stubborn and babyish. Guys certainly didn't tell girls they liked *that*. All at once she remembered Jonathan's eyes, the look in his eyes when he first saw her. Oh, he had liked her then. When she first saw him, she had liked him, too. She swallowed hard and clenched her fist under the table. There was no denying, they had been attracted to each other at first sight. But the minute they stopped looking at each other and started talking, fireworks — the wrong kind of fireworks — had gone off. Fiona forced herself to remember exactly how awful her day had been: the cold, the rain, the miserable football game, Jonathan's sappy jokes. It had been a disaster. When she looked up again, she was in control. She met Holly's questioning gaze squarely: "I can't say one way or another whether he liked the company. He's a nice guy, but I don't think I'd go out with him again. Besides, I have no time for guys right now. Not with the show coming up so soon."

Fiona thought she sounded pretty convincing as she said that. Then she launched into her latest ideas for staging the dance numbers in the show. Soon no one was talking about football or Jonathan and Fiona anymore.

# *Chapter*
# *9*

Fiona toweled the beads of sweat off her back and chest, and quickly slipped a flannel shirt over her leotard. "Good work, guys. I think you got the right idea now," she said, giving the boys on stage at Kennedy's Little Theater an encouraging smile. She went down the side stairs leading into the aisle, where Ms. Everson and Woody were sitting talking to Michael at the piano.

"Did you like that?" she asked Ms. Everson, tugging up her red leg warmers. It was late Monday afternoon and Fiona had just demonstrated her solution to the problem of the male dancers for *Oklahoma!* The guys auditioning for dance roles had proved really hopeless. But while watching them, Fiona had a brainstorm. As she had explained to Ms. Everson, the show had everything to do with cow*boys*, so substituting girls in the dance numbers wouldn't work. But using the boys as extras would.

"I love it!" Ms. Everson approved.

"It's a whole new concept — living props!" Woody joked.

"The guys are not props!" Fiona purposely ignored Woody's humor. Woody was supposed to be the play's director, not resident stand-up comic. She just couldn't understand his flippant attitude. He was setting such a bad example for the rest of the cast. Fiona didn't think Woody'd be able to pull the show together in the next couple of weeks. She wasn't sure she could either, but she was determined to try. She couldn't bear the thought of failing at one more thing. It was up to her to teach this spirited group of players to move like dancers and get the ballet scenes to work. For starters she was going to set a serious, hard-working tone to these rehearsals. "In opera and ballet production, they're called *extras*," Fiona informed Woody. She turned to Ms. Everson and added, "The girls can dance around the guys who'll be posing and strolling around the stage. Parts of *Rodeo* are like that. That was choreographed by Agnes DeMille, too."

Woody whistled. "I'm impressed. If Aggie can do it, so can we! I was thinking, though — "

Fiona disregarded Woody and barreled on. "The next problem are the leads, Laurie and Ado Annie." She turned to Michael. "We could cut the music here, and here." Fiona showed him Phoebe's copy of the score and explained her ideas for using Phoebe and Elise Hammond as dancers *and* singers. "That way we only have one big ballet number."

Fiona looked toward Ms. Everson for approval. Ms. Everson looked toward Woody. Woody grinned. "Sounds great to me."

"I really think you should have a free hand in all this. After all, you are the dance pro around here," Ms. Everson said, checking her watch. "I've got to go now, but I'll leave it up to you and Woody to work out the details for dance rehearsals and full cast calls. Michael will set up some singing sessions with the leads to smooth things out on the music end." She turned to the stage and addressed the cast. "I just want to remind everybody that opening night is less than two weeks away. I know *Oklahoma!* wasn't everyone's first choice for a Holiday production — "

A chorus of assents interrupted the drama coach's statement. Woody jumped up on his seat and gave a mighty yell. Everyone, including Fiona, jumped. "But the good news is we're practically sold out already for opening night. In fact the Kennedy Players are probably going to be the top contributors to Jonathan's Holiday Homeless Drive." Woody dramatically patted himself on the back. "I'd like to take a little credit for that."

At the mention of Jonathan's name, Fiona looked up. She had practically forgotten the play had anything to do with him. Except for their heated exchange about missing out on The Barn Dance Saturday afternoon, neither of them had mentioned the show at all. It was hard to believe the same guy she went out with over the weekend was capable of dreaming up a scheme for helping the homeless in the area. The guy who took her to the game didn't seem like the kind of person who could get anything done. Jonathan reminded her of Woody somehow. Always clowning around.

Ms. Everson joined in the laughter and congratulations following Woody's announcement. "Webster, as usual, has stolen my thunder," the coach chuckled. "I just wanted to say . . . I know this is a pretty tough musical for you kids to put on. But I have absolute confidence you've all got what it takes to make a real blockbuster of a show." With that, she waved good-bye, and hurried out the door of the old colonial chapel that served as Kennedy High's Little Theater.

Fiona pulled off her shirt and tugged down the back of her leotard. "Hey, where's everyone going?" she cried, bouncing back up the steps to the stage. Bart was packing up his guitar, and Elise was pulling her jeans on over her tights. Phoebe was still kneeling by the footlights talking to Michael. The rest of the cast was gathering up their coats and books.

"Home," Elise said innocently. "I've got a huge test tomorrow."

"And I'm starved." Bart patted his firm stomach. "I'm going to the sub shop — anybody want to join me?"

Fiona stared at the group in disbelief. "Didn't you chaps hear what Ms. Everson just said? We've got almost no time to get this show together. Just because she left for a faculty meeting doesn't mean rehearsals break up. When we had shows at Kingsmont we rehearsed all night."

"What?" Elise shrieked. "My parents sure wouldn't go for that."

"Neither would the principal!" Michael laughed, then turned to Fiona. "That won't work here at Kennedy. I'm afraid the night custodian would kill us."

"I didn't mean we should stay here all night, but there's still a lot more work to be done this afternoon. Another hour won't kill anyone," Fiona said firmly. She looked at the cast members. Everyone shifted uncomfortably.

"It's pretty late already, Fiona." Phoebe scrambled to her feet and approached Jeremy's sister. "And I've got a ton of homework plus some college applications to get out. Besides, I sort of thought we were done for today." Phoebe turned to Woody with a puzzled look on her face. "The songs went well, didn't they? Maybe just the dancers should stay."

"That won't work," Fiona said. She strode to center stage and faced Phoebe head on. "You need to stay; so does Elise. All the girls need to stay. You've got to start working on the steps to one of the numbers tonight. If I teach them to you now, you can rehearse them at home."

"At home?" Elise's jaw dropped.

"You rehearse your lines and songs at home. Dancing is just as important," Fiona said passionately. She paced up and down the stage, the color rising in her cheeks. She stopped in front of Bart. He was tall and brawny and towered over her.

Bart took a couple of startled steps backward as Fiona said in a no-nonsense voice, "If you were practicing for a football game right now, you wouldn't have time to be thinking about your stomach and the sub shop. Dance takes just as much work as football — maybe even more. If you want to be in the show, you have to sweat to make it a success." When Fiona finished her little speech, there was silence in the auditorium.

"Bravo!" Michael finally cheered from down by the piano. Phoebe stared at him in disbelief. She looked past Michael toward Woody, who was grinning broadly and nodding in agreement.

Suddenly everyone began talking and arguing at once. No one wanted to stay. Woody jumped onto the stage and shouted, "Quiet!" Everyone fell silent. He checked the clock, then shoved his fists into his pockets and looked around at the cast. "Fiona's right," he finally said. "The music numbers did go well. Same goes for the dialogue and individual scenes. But we need to get the whole thing put together and staged properly. That means the dance stuff has to be worked on. Fiona needs the whole cast here for that." Woody paused and eyed the solemn group before him. "And that's the way it's going to be from here on in." Fiona gave Woody a grateful look.

There was a lot of grumbling as everyone dumped their books, took off their coats, and climbed back up on the stage. Woody approached Bart and lightly punched him in the arm. "Fiona was too polite to say anything, my man, but the opener looked pretty wimpy last time you did it.

How about running through it one more time while Fiona organizes the girls for their dances?"

Bart groaned, but unpacked his guitar and slung it over his shoulder. He shoved his cowboy hat back on his head and strode across the stage. A minute later his warm baritone voice rang out into the empty auditorium.

# Chapter
# 10

Woody Webster was about to explode. For the past hour he had watched Fiona work with the cast. Nothing seemed to be going smoothly, and Phoebe looked like she was about to burst into tears. From his seat in the middle of the auditorium, Woody wasn't sure he should interfere. His instincts said Fiona was right on target, pushing the girls until they began to shape up and look like dancers. But he really felt badly for Phoebe.

"Phoebe, that's the tenth time I've showed you that combination of steps," Fiona steamed. She had her hands on her hips.

"I can't help it if I'm not a dancer!" Phoebe retorted. She shoved her hands into the pockets of her old pink overalls and shook her head. Her cheeks were flushed from dancing under the lights.

Woody wasn't sure how much more of this he

could watch. He got up and moved slowly toward the stage.

"You don't have to be a dancer to do these steps right. It's just one-two-three, hop, slide-two-three, hop." Fiona demonstrated as she spoke, making the sequence look simple. Phoebe and Fiona were about the same height but Phoebe had a sturdier, more solid build, and somehow looked shorter and heavier standing behind the small-boned, straight-backed dancer. "You're very musical and you move well naturally," Fiona declared. "I know you can do it."

"Obviously I don't move well enough," she mumbled uncooperatively.

Fiona tossed aside her notepad and marched up to Phoebe. She grabbed the red head by the shoulders and gave her a gentle shake. "Phoebe Hall, if you'd only stand up straighter, get those hands out of your pockets and *feel* like you're a dancer, you'd look like one." Fiona stepped back and took a long look at Phoebe. "And those overalls don't help. *Real* dancers wouldn't wear something like that to rehearsal."

"What's wrong with my overalls!" Phoebe gasped, taking her hands out of the fraying pockets.

"Imagine yourself back in the era of this musical. Girls didn't wear overalls. Not the girls guys were courting. A grungy cowpunch comes off the range — " Fiona had really done her homework over the weekend. She knew just how Curly would act, how Laurie should look. She swaggered across the stage, slightly bowed. She

99

moved exactly like Bart, then stopped and struck a very feminine pose. "You're everything he longs for — sweet, fresh and pretty. You've got to be a vision of femininity." Fiona made a frilly sort of gesture with her hands. Bart whistled under his breath. "So that's what I'm supposed to like. Dresses. Frilly girls. Wait until Holly hears this!"

Phoebe rolled her eyes. "You've got to be kidding."

Her sarcasm went right past Fiona. "No. It's really quite simple. You need to have a skirt on."

"Well, I'm not wearing these for the performance, you know," Phoebe said, her voice rising.

Fiona cleared her throat. "I know that. But you have to get used to moving in a skirt. You're not getting the right feeling in overalls. Wear a full-ish skirt tomorrow to practice — it'll help you move better. At Kingsmont, we used to always rehearse in skirts once we knew the basic steps. You get a better sense of the movement."

Before Phoebe could protest, Fiona started counting out the music. "Michael, take it from the top, one more time. Now, "Many a fine day will — " Fiona half sang, half spoke the words to the tune, and danced in front of Phoebe and the chorus of girls.

Her voice was about a mile off-key. Phoebe winced. She wanted absolutely no part of this nonsense. Song and dance numbers should be fun, not torture. She started off the stage then spotted Woody standing by the orchestra pit. It was hard to see past the footlights but two other people were sitting in the last row. Phoebe hated the idea of looking like a fool, especially in front of her friends .She marched back to her place in front of the other girls and tried to remember how she felt wearing her favorite summer skirt. Making the cheesiest smile she could, Phoebe started dancing. This time she got through the first section of the dance perfectly.

"Smashing!" Fiona clapped her hands and came up to Phoebe when the music was finished. "You were great. That's it. Now try to remember the way you felt dancing like that." The critical tone was gone from her voice. She sounded warm, enthusiastic, and really proud.

Phoebe tensed up slightly. "Uh — thanks," she said, and backed away.

Fiona didn't notice Phoebe's reaction. She had just looked out to the audience. Jeremy was hurrying down the center aisle toward her with Jonathan right behind him, his old hat shoved back on his head. What in the world was Jonathan doing here? Fiona swallowed hard and turned toward the rest of the girls. She grabbed a towel and said "I think we're all beat now. Let's call it a day, but try to work on these steps tonight. Go over them in front of your mirrors at home. They'll feel easier tomorrow." Fiona dismissed the group, and grabbed her dance bag. "Good work, Phoebe," she said over her shoulder, but Phoebe was already in the orchestra pit, pulling on her pea coat. Woody barreled up the steps to the stage.

"I'm impressed, Fiona," he congratulated.

"You had me worried there for a minute."

"Worried?" Fiona asked, trying to watch Jonathan out of the corner of her eye. Jeremy was snapping pictures of Elise and Bart as they clowned around, practicing one of the easy lifts Fiona had just taught them.

"That you'd have the whole crew in tears. I was about to find the custodian so he could mop up the flood," Woody joked, looking back at Phoebe. She was perched on top of the piano and she looked like she had been crying.

Fiona followed Woody's gaze and heaved a sigh. "I always ended up crying during rehearsals. Everyone did back home. But the only way to get people to perform their best is to push them. I really believe that. We don't have time to coddle the cast if we want to put a really professional show together," Fiona stated, yanking off her leg-warmers.

Michael walked up. "I'll second that," he said, thumping Woody on the shoulder. "Like Woody said the other night, now that we have a real pro on the team, we might get our show on the road."

"Fiona!" Jeremy waved as he vaulted onto the stage. Jonathan was climbing the far stairs. Fiona waved at Jeremy, then smiled hesitantly at Jonathan. Why did he have to be so handsome? The glare from the footlights blinded her a bit, and she couldn't quite see his eyes. She wondered how long he'd been watching her. She pulled a comb out of her dance bag, and tugged it through her tangled hair.

"Hey Preston, have I got news! We're sold out

for opening night!" Woody whooped, and jogged over to Jonathan. The two of them headed back stage. Fiona felt relieved. He had probably turned up to talk to Woody about money. He hadn't come to see her dance at all.

Jeremy walked up to his sister and affectionately tousled her hair.

"How long have you been here?" Fiona asked.

"Long enough to see you start making these kids look like dancers." Jeremy lowered his voice and slung his arm around his sister. He led her downstage, away from the cast and crew. "You know," he confided, "I've never seen anyone *move* as good as you. Even Phoebe looked clumsy compared to you — and she's a pretty awesome dancer."

Fiona instantly defended Phoebe. "Phoebe hasn't got a clumsy bone in her body. She was terrific today. Besides," she shot an accusing look at her brother, "I don't know what the big deal is about me looking so good or doing so well. After all, Jeremy, I am a trained dancer."

Jeremy looked hurt. "I just think you're doing a good job. Last week you said you didn't know a thing about musicals and today you seem to be running this show."

"Well, it went okay," she admitted, "but that's just one day. I haven't begun to work out the hard parts. Why don't you wait until opening night to congratulate me, Jeremy," she said, wondering if congratulations would be in order when *Oklahoma!* finally premiered. Fiona shook off that thought. If she let herself think the show

103

would bomb, it would. She remembered once hearing someone say if you thought you might fail at something, chances were pretty good that you would. Thinking you could do something, no matter how tough and impossible it seemed, meant you were that much closer to doing it well. Fiona wasn't quite sure she believed that anymore. She had been completely confident she'd get into the National Ballet, but she had failed anyway.

Fiona shook her short hair off her face and forced herself to stand tall. She was stretching her arms high over her head, trying to release the sudden tension she felt in the back of her neck, when Bart strolled up and whispered in her ear.

"M'am," he drawled. "You think me and you and the rest of the crew might partake in some vittles at the sub shop now?"

Fiona inched away from Bart, and shook her head. He was supposedly Holly's steady guy, but he always seemed to be flirting. Fiona didn't know how Holly stood for it. "No," she finally answered.

"I thought you said if I danced a hole in these here boots I could eat." Bart's face sagged with disappointment.

"Did I really say *that*?" Fiona laughed in spite of herself. "Rehearsal's over, everyone can do what they want, I guess."

"Class dismissed," Bart cheered, tossing his Stetson up in the air. "Miz Stone says we can go play now at the sub shop. Anyone want to join in the fun?"

Bart jumped off the stage, followed by the rowdy, liberated cast.

*　*　*

Fiona moved swiftly across the empty stage of the half-lit theatre. "Out of My Dreams" was playing on the tape recorder, and as Fiona danced she became Laurie, the pretty ranch girl who pretended she didn't like cowboy Curly at all. Then the mood of the music changed to dark and ominous. Curly's rival, Judd, was supposed to dance into Laurie's dream. Fiona spun to a halt and stamped her foot. "Drat! Why can't I get it?" She couldn't figure out Judd's dance, and she had been working for over an hour now.

Fiona shoved the terrycloth headband up on her forehead and went over to the recorder. As she bent down and pressed rewind, a voice called from the darkened audience. "Didn't anyone ever tell you all work and no play made Jill a dull girl?"

Fiona jumped slightly. She peered into the back of the theatre. Jonathan Preston was sitting on the arm of an aisle seat jangling a bunch of car keys in his hand.

"Uh — what are you doing here?" she stammered. "How — how'd you know I was here?"

Jonathan didn't say why he was there. He simply announced, "I just came from the sub shop. Woody told me you were still here. It's past six, you know. The last school bus left forty minutes ago. How are you getting home?" He hopped up onto the stage and propped his long body against a sawhorse. When he looked at Fiona, his gray eyes were serious. "That was a nice dance." After a second he added shyly, "I thought you looked wonderful."

Fiona's hand flew into her hair, and she glanced away from Jonathan in confusion. She *knew* she was a mess. She scampered over to the outlet and unplugged her cassette player. "I sort of lost track of time. I guess I'll walk home," she mumbled into the wings.

"Walk!" Jonathan exclaimed. "It's pouring out — and dark." Then he snapped his fingers together. "Whoops, I forgot. I'm talking to a girl who loves getting wet and doesn't mind the cold at all."

Fiona looked up quickly. "That's unfair," she said icily. Jonathan wasn't only being unfair in referring to their disastrous date, he was being tactless. She was about to tell him so when she spotted a playful smile on his face. She looked at him for a long time, then she smiled, too.

"Guess I deserved that." She wanted to say more, but she had never been good at apologies, so, instead, she pulled on her shirt, grabbed her jacket and dance bag and started down the side stairs. "The city buses are still running, aren't they?" she asked suddenly in a worried voice.

"They run all night, but I thought you might need a ride." He stood up straight and stretched. Fiona watched him in amazement. He looked tall as a tree. The idea of Jonathan being a tree made her laugh. He laughed back and jangled his car keys in front of her. "Big Pink is ready, willing, and able."

Before she could stop herself, Fiona blurted out, "My last encounter with your car was anything but warm and dry. I might as well walk."

Jonathan threw up his arms in defeat. "Touché! I guess I deserved that!" He scrambled down the stairs and followed Fiona toward the door. "Except now the heater works!" he announced proudly. "My friend Matt and I fixed it Saturday night."

Fiona's eyebrows shot up. As she pushed open the front door of the theatre and switched off the lights, she said, "So *that's* the 'more important thing' you had to do on Saturday. Muck around with a car?"

She turned around, expecting to hear Jonathan's comeback. One looked at his face and her own smile vanished.

Jonathan's eyes were smoldering. "You shouldn't put down things you don't understand. Didn't anyone ever tell you that?" Jonathan snapped angrily. He stomped down the steps of the theater ahead of Fiona into the rain. Fiona ran after him.

"What are you talking about?" She grabbed his arm and forced him to face her. Touching Jonathan was an impulsive, angry gesture but its effect was overpowering. A feeling of incredible warmth engulfed her and time seemed to stop. She forgot all about being angry. She forgot about the rain and that her feet were in a puddle. She was lost in Jonathan's eyes. For a very long second they stood like that: face-to-face on the walk outside the chapel. Jonathan's expression softened.

*Oh, no. He's going to kiss me!* Fiona suddenly realized, and the dreamy feeling vanished. She

107

abruptly dropped his arm and began marching through the parking lot to his car. Jonathan clenched his fists and ran after her. The rain was heavy, and the wind bitter, but Fiona's cheeks were hot. "I don't know what you're being so huffy about. Why should someone like me understand cars?"

"Just because you don't like them doesn't mean everyone else shouldn't, too," Jonathan sputtered. He flung open the door to his Chevy. Fiona tossed her bag on the front seat and climbed in. This time she snagged her leggings on an old upholstery spring. Jonathan slammed her door shut and Fiona stared broodingly at her hands. They were clasped tightly in her lap. She swallowed hard and closed her eyes. Why did she have to fight with Jonathan every time she ran into him? A wave of guilt washed over her. She had just remembered Dee telling her Jonathan got along with everybody. It must be her own fault.

Jonathan opened his door and jammed the key into the ignition. Out of the corner of her eye she could see his jaw was set and a small vein in his temple was throbbing.

"I guess I don't understand about cars *or* guys. I'm sorry," Fiona said.

"I'm not talking about cars," Jonathan said, keeping his eyes on the traffic. Fiona bit her lip. Somehow she knew that, even before he said it.

When they came to a stoplight, he turned toward her. His eyes weren't angry anymore, but they were still very serious. "Why are you so angry all the time?" he asked.

"I'm not angry!" she retorted, meeting his intense gaze head on. Neither of them looked away until the car behind them honked.

Jonathan began to smile, as he turned his attention back to the road. "If you're not mad now, I wonder what you're like when you're really fuming."

Fiona squirmed in her seat. "Awful," she said bluntly. "My roommate Elizabeth told me that. We fought a lot."

Jonathan startled Fiona by throwing his head back and laughing. "Thanks for the warning."

Fiona looked out her window, feeling very embarrassed. Finally she said, "I *am* sorry, you know. I apologize. For today — and for Saturday. I didn't mean to be so — "

"Angry?" Jonathan supplied with a smile. "Me, too. I'm sorry. So far we haven't been communicating very well."

Fiona looked up and realized they weren't heading for her house. "Hey, where are we going?"

"The sub shop. Some of the cast is still there. I'm starved. I went over looking for you and drove right back to school to rescue you from a severe case of overexertion."

Discovering that Jonathan had gone to the sub shop just to find her made Fiona uncomfortable. "No, I want to go home. It really is late. I have more work to do before rehearsal tomorrow, and homework."

Jonathan frowned. "Didn't anyone ever tell you there's a right time to work and a right time to spend getting to know people?"

"You just don't understand," Fiona said tightly. "If you love your work, you don't mind doing it twenty-four hours a day."

"Maybe the people around you mind — try thinking about that."

"Why should I?" Fiona said defensively, folding her arms across her chest. Jonathan's remark bothered her. She had always worked like a demon to get what she wanted. Nothing was wrong with that and she thought it was one of her better qualities.

Jonathan chuckled. "We're not communicating again."

"I guess we're not," Fiona said, a note of disappointment in her voice. She tucked her feet under her on the seat and stared out the window. The rest of the ride through the rain was quiet except for Fiona humming an off-key version of "People Will Say We're in Love."

Jonathan's deep voice broke the silence. They were almost at her house when he asked, "What's that you're singing?" Fiona couldn't see his face but his question sounded innocent enough.

She blushed in the dark. "Oh," she said as casually as she could. "Just a tune from the show I've got to think of steps to."

# Chapter
## 11

Phoebe Hall sat in the sub shop booth poking her straw in and out of an empty can of diet soda. Her resentment and anger had been building up ever since she left rehearsal. Maybe she was being unfair to Fiona. Michael thought Fiona was doing a great job of putting the show in order. Phoebe tried as hard as she could to see today's rehearsal from his point of view, because she didn't want this discussion to turn into an argument. But she was convinced that Michael was wrong. Woody was wrong, too. But Phoebe knew she wasn't the only member of the cast who was dreading the next rehearsal.

"I guess," she finally said, "I just don't agree."

"Pheeberooni, how can you disagree? All we're saying is that Fiona's a pro," Woody repeated patiently. "And that she conducted a really professional rehearsal."

"That's not the point," Phoebe said hotly. "The point is I'm not a pro — yet. Neither is Bart, or Elise, or Tommy, or anyone else in the show. We're only high school kids, and we're doing the best we can."

"Come on, Phoebe. You know it takes a lot of work to pull a musical together," Michael said. "You've been in shows before."

Phoebe slapped her hand on the tabletop. "Yes. I know I have. And I've been successful in them before, too. That's why I resent being treated the way I was today."

Woody jumped to Fiona's defense. "That's not fair, Phoebe. Fiona's just working hard. She's intense and driven, but she was full of praise whenever something went well. She just wanted you — everyone — to take the rehearsal seriously."

Bart interrupted. "Sure, Woody. Except she's not the director, *you* are. And she was pushing us as if we were about to open at Kennedy Center next week. We do have the rest of our lives to lead. Tell me," Bart leaned back in his seat and asked the rest of the table, "Who really has the time to go home tonight and dance for three hours in front of their mirrors? I've got a physics test tomorrow."

"Right on, Bart!" Elise cheered. She turned to Woody and put on her coat. "Phoebe's right, you know. Until today, rehearsals have been going well. Most of the show is in really good shape. And it's been a lot of fun working on it. But today — " Elise broke off and summed up her

112

feelings with a disgusted thumbs-down gesture. "Well, I agree with Phoebe. I've got to get going. See you later." She reached down the long table and gave Phoebe's arm a supportive squeeze, then ran out of the sub shop to catch her ride home.

Phoebe let out a sigh and slid down in her seat. She twiddled her thumbs and stared intently at her hands. "It sounds like I'm on a 'dump on Fiona' kick, and I'm not. I just figured that since this is probably the last play I'll be in at Kennedy, I want to enjoy it. I don't want to feel like I'm in basic training," she grumbled.

Woody cracked up. "It did look that way, didn't it? I never thought such a delicate-looking girl could sound like a drill sergeant."

Michael grinned and tugged at his thick dark hair. "Actually, Pheeb, maybe it is basic training," he teased, but Phoebe could tell he was at least half-serious as he said, "Next year when you go to college and major in music and theatre, Fiona's workouts are going to seem like nothing."

Before Phoebe could respond, Holly walked in, followed by Jeremy and Diana. Holly plopped herself down next to Bart and greeted the crowd. "Guess what?" she announced. "I definitely, positively and absolutely won't have to work at the clinic the night *Oklahoma!* opens." Holly's social life had been cramped the past few weeks because of her work on the evening shift at the medical clinic at Rose Hill Hospital.

Bart sighed with relief and buried his face in Holly's hair. "So, the boss finally broke down."

"Come off it, Bart," she giggled. "Dr. Ellerbee's

a cardiologist — he's all heart."

"That's *bad* — really bad," Woody groaned. "Take it from a professional punster, you'd better stick to medicine, Ms. Daniels."

Jeremy and Diana settled down at the end of the table. Jeremy scanned the room. "Hey, what'd you do with Fiona?" He peered under the table, then inside Woody's empty soda container.

Woody and Phoebe exchanged a tense glance. Michael laughed easily. "Everyone seems to be looking for Fiona. Jonathan was looking for her a while ago. Maybe *he* knows where she danced off to."

Jeremy flashed Diana an "I told you so" kind of look and said, "I know she's my sister, but that's the first time I ever saw her really work. I think she has what it takes to get this old musical off the ground. Don't you guys?"

Michael cast a warning glance at Phoebe, and Bart eyed Jeremy skeptically. Jeremy didn't notice. He was leaning forward listening to Woody's response.

"Your sister, old chap, is a real pro. And she is helping this thing take shape tremendously," Woody said, making a mental note to talk to Fiona. She *was* a pro. She was doing a great job. But maybe she could ease up just a bit. He had never seen his players so upset. And the toughest week of rehearsals was coming up. Well, he *was* the director, and it was up to him to steer clear of a storm. Unfortunately, his instincts told him a storm was brewing just around the corner.

* * *

Fiona sat cross-legged in the middle of her huge four-poster bed apologizing to Dee on the phone. She had stood Dee up at dancercise class and she had no excuse. She had gotten so caught up in the rehearsal and working out the "Out of My Dreams" sequence afterward, she had simply forgotten.

Apologizing made her think of Jonathan and their conversation on the way home. She had an uncomfortable feeling that a lot of what he said about her not understanding people, about her working too hard, and hurting people around her was true. Thinking about Jonathan made her head ache slightly. She pressed her fingers to her temples and closed her eyes. Finally she said, "Dee, I promise I won't do it again."

"So, you'll come next week then?" Dee asked hopefully. Dee was her closest friend here in Rose Hill. She didn't want to disappoint her again. "No. I can't promise that, Dee," Fiona said truthfully, hoping Dee would understand. "I have to wait until this show is over. I didn't realize how much work it would be."

"Well, I'll miss you, but I understand," Dee replied. "Tell me how rehearsal went."

"Oh, Dee," Fiona burst out. "I'm so scared." She was suddenly grateful there was someone she could talk to. "I think I'm getting the feel for the dancing, but no one in the cast is a real dancer, and even *with* real dancers, ten days is impossible — "

"Every show they've had at Kennedy is like that," Dee broke in. "I was talking to Michael about it the other night at Monica's. Somehow Woody manages to pull it together. A lot of bloopers happen, but that's half the fun."

"Bloopers? You mean *mistakes*?" Fiona was astounded. "This show can't have mistakes in it. I want it to look really professional." Fiona resisted an impulse to tell Dee that no show was worth doing unless you tried to make it perfect. Again she thought about Jonathan, and how she fought with him. She didn't want to fight with Dee. She flopped down onto the mound of pillows at the head of her bed, and began stretching her legs in the air as she talked.

"Actually, I feel funny asking you this — after standing you up — " Fiona started.

"Hey, forget it. I understand. The artist got lost in her work," Dee said good-naturedly. "So what's up?"

"If you and Marc aren't busy Wednesday, do you think we could all go to that cowboy dance club I told you about? I really need to see some folk and square dances to choreograph the closing number, and this will be my last chance before the show opens."

"I'd love to!" Dee exclaimed. "In fact," she added after a pause, "Why not invite the whole cast? It would be fun. We could organize a bunch of cars."

Fiona sat up on the mattress. "Dee Patterson, you're a genius." After they made their plans,

Fiona hung up the phone, and sprawled face-down on her bed. Suddenly, she had a wonderful feeling that there was a ray of hope, one slight chance in a million, that the show might go well after all.

She glanced across her room at the poster of Baryshnikov hanging over her desk. She wondered if great choreographers had problems getting shows together. For a second her heart stopped. If she had passed the audition in London, she would be working professionally now herself. There'd be no question of making something good enough for a high school show. She'd be busy making something perfect enough to be performed at an opera house. She hadn't let herself think about that — there hadn't been enough time.

She began to daydream about meeting Baryshnikov: What it would be like walking up to him, talking to him, asking him all the questions she wanted to ask about how to make a performance tick. Fiona rolled over on her back and stared at the high ceiling, trying to visualize Baryshnikov. He wasn't very tall, but he was so intense and romantic. She closed her eyes and pictured him in an empty dance studio, a big, sun-filled room with strains from the *pas de deux* from *Romeo and Juliet*. He would notice her in the mirror doing her stretches and he would approach her silently and say in his exotic accent, "Dance with me."

But something was wrong with the picture in

Fiona's mind. Standing next to her, Baryshnikov suddenly became tall as a tree, and his accent went from Russian to American. His hand felt familiar and reassuring and the music playing wasn't Tchaikovsky, it was a song from *Oklahoma!* As he put his hand around her waist, she looked up into his eyes, and they were gray not blue. Baryshnikov had turned into Jonathan.

# Chapter 12

"If you guys ever need a job, there's one waiting at Garfield," Tony Martinez said to Jonathan and Matt, as he surveyed the basement. A few Garfield kids were still sweeping up the sawdust. The rest of the Fix-It Club and the Kennedy volunteers had long since gone. They had all met at Garfield House that evening to clean out the basement, and start building storage bins for the Homeless Drive donations.

"I might just take you up on that," Matt grinned, slipping on his leather jacket.

"Actually we're in the middle of a job right now, aren't we?" Jonathan reminded. "The Homeless Drive has just begun. Matt will start bringing donations over from Kennedy tomorrow."

Jonathan looked around and sighed. He was proud of the hard work the kids had done tonight.

And he had done more than his fair share of drilling, toting lumber, and carting away heavy trash bags. But all the hard work in the world wouldn't take his mind off Fiona. All he could think about was how beautiful she looked standing outside the chapel in the rain, her face turned up toward his. For a minute, he almost believed she would have let him — no, she wanted him to — kiss her.

The rain had stopped, and clouds scudded across the full moon. Jonathan's shoulders tightened from the cold as the two boys left Garfield House and climbed into Matt's pickup truck. They were halfway to Jonathan's house before Matt broke the silence.

"Things aren't working out so well with that girl, are they?" Matt asked.

"What girl?" Jonathan said, then pulled his hat down over his face and stared out the window. "You mean Fiona?"

"The girl you took to the football game. Jeremy Stone's sister."

"No. Nothing's working. I really took her just to be polite. But Matt," Jonathan straightened up and practically whispered, "She's beautiful. I took one look at her and. . . ."

"And — " Matt urged Jonathan to continue.

Jonathan relaxed. "She isn't interested, I guess. I'm not sure. Everytime I see her, we fight. We fought all day Saturday. This evening, I thought I'd give it another try. I went to the play rehearsal. Afterward, we fought again. She's incredibly hostile." He filled Matt in on the details of Saturday's disastrous outing.

"You should forget her. Sounds like she's pretty self-centered, Jonathan. That's not the kind of girl you usually like," Matt said.

Jonathan studied his hands. Fiona was the most temperamental, hardheaded girl he had ever met. He looked straight ahead out of the windshield, and tried to sort through the confused feelings he had for her. The wet pavement shimmered beneath the streetlights and the bare trees swayed in the gusty wind. Jonathan suddenly realized that wild, wet rainy days would always remind him of Fiona. At the football game Saturday she had looked so tiny, and so terribly cold, and miserable. But she had acted tough and distant. And even in spite of that she had managed to look incredibly beautiful. All he wanted was to gather her up in his arms and protect her from the cold, from anything that might hurt her. But he couldn't — not then — or now. She was determined to fight whatever battle she was fighting all by herself. The problem was, Jonathan couldn't quite figure out what the war inside Fiona was all about.

"I can't forget her. And I think you're wrong. She's not self-centered. She's just led a sheltered life. She's only seen a very small part of the world. Fiona doesn't know what exists beyond ballet school and her dancer friends."

"She must feel like she's landed on Mars," Matt commented. "Kennedy's a pretty big school with

121

lots of different kinds of kids. It's probably tough on her."

"It is, but there's something else. You should have seen her today at that rehearsal. She was so hard on everyone. And she's even harder on herself. I watched her dance for twenty minutes on that empty stage. Fiona kept going over the same steps again and again, trying to make them perfect. She's so driven."

Matt parked at the curb outside Jonathan's house. "I've met guys like that. Usually they've got some ax of their own to grind. My guess is, Fiona's terrified the show won't come off. She's scared to death she'll blow it." Matt stretched and rolled his neck to get the kinks out. "I bet Fiona's pretty sweet underneath that hard surface," he added as an afterthought. Jonathan stifled a smile. Girls he knew had said the same thing about Matt Jacobs. Jonathan shoved his hat back and opened the truck door. If Fiona was at all like Matt in that way, maybe there was hope. Matt was his best friend, but he was a hard guy to get to know. He had had some hard knocks when he was a kid and he seldom talked about it. But beneath his macho shell he had a heart of gold. Jonathan slammed the door shut and leaned against the half-opened window.

"I don't know, Matt. I only know I'm in love with her, and I don't know what to do about it."

"Keep trying," Matt shouted out the window as he pulled away.

Jonathan watched Matt's truck turn the corner,

then opened the wooden gate. "Hi, Sherlock," he laughed, greeting his droopy-eared hound. He looked up to the sound of his mother's typewriter. The whole house was dark except for the round attic window where he could see his mother's profile as she banged away at a new mystery novel. His sister Kate was long asleep, and his father was away at a mathematics conference. "What a crazy family, Sherlock," he said, tickling the dog behind his silky ears.

Jonathan hesitated before going into the house. His mother would hear him and come downstairs. They'd have some hot chocolate and laugh about her latest plot. Jonathan didn't want to go in yet. He needed to be alone for a minute to sort out his thoughts. Jonathan sat down on the wet swing seat that hung from the apple tree in the front lawn. He swung gently while Sherlock sniffed at the base of the tree. Matt was probably right. Fiona was terrified of failing again, and she wasn't really angry — just hurting. To protect herself she had set up a shield. He wanted so badly to help her. Well, Jonathan wasn't about to give up. Fiona was unlike any girl he had ever met before. . . . And he had fallen completely in love with her the moment he first saw her.

# Chapter
## 13

Fiona stood just inside the open double doors of The Barn Dance, shaking the snow from her hair, and waiting for Woody. After today's rehearsal, Woody had said he needed to talk to her about the show. There had been no chance during the trip to Maryville in Michael's van: everyone was singing Christmas carols to celebrate the first real snowfall of the season. Fiona had hummed along, enjoying the ride through the dark countryside north of Rose Hill. But at the same time, she wondered if the cast was really going to learn anything at tonight's country dancing session. Woody's crowd had a habit of turning every gathering into a party. Well, Fiona was going to The Barn Dance to work, and that's exactly what she intended to do.

She had expected the Maryville club to be

empty on a Wednesday night, instead it was packed to the rafters. Otherwise the place was exactly as she had imagined it: wooden, big, and very warm. Near the entrance was a fire in the huge brick and stone fireplace. On the stage at the far end of the converted barn, a country music band was playing a lively tune. Fiona couldn't wait to start dancing.

Woody walked back from the coatcheck and guided Fiona inside the main room where Bart, Holly, Kim, Phoebe, and Michael were already gathered around one of the tables. Marc and Dee and the rest of the crew hadn't turned up yet.

Woody steered Fiona away from the crowd's table and over to a far corner of the dance floor down by the stage. He pulled up a bench and she sat down while he went for sodas.

"How did you think rehearsal went today?" Woody asked when he got back to the table.

The question surprised Fiona. He really hadn't said much about the show to her except during rehearsals. Even then he had mainly sat back and watched her try to shape the staging and dance numbers to her liking. And he clowned around, of course, and joked with the cast between numbers. Fiona had started to wonder if he was interested in the show at all. "I guess it went fine," Fiona said sipping her soda. "No, actually, it didn't," she contradicted herself a moment later. "No one's working hard enough, Woody." She considered her next words carefully. She was annoyed at him for being such a joker. "And I think if *you* had a more serious attitude, people would push themselves harder. The kids look up to you."

Woody gaped at Fiona. "Whew!" he whistled, and leaned back against the wall. He drank some Coke and fiddled with his suspenders. Then he cleared his throat. "Fiona, I didn't come here to talk about me and the show. I'll think about what you said, though. Maybe I should act more serious when I play director." He leaned forward and propped his elbows on the table, his chin in his hands. He stared at the whirling circles of dancers and drummed his fingers against his cheek.

Finally he forced his eyes off the dance floor and back to Fiona. "I sort of wanted to suggest something."

Fiona cocked her head, and eyed Woody suspiciously.

"I think you should back down a bit during rehearsals."

"Back down?" Fiona was sure she had misunderstood him. "You mean not push as hard?"

"Precisely. Murmurs of rebellion have been heard among the troops."

Fiona jumped up. "You're crazy, Woody. I just told you no one's working hard enough. Don't you care about this show?"

"I care very much about this show, Fiona," Woody declared. "That's why you'd better back down. The cast is chafing at the bit. There's trouble brewing, and too much depends on the success of this show to blow it."

"How can you suggest *I'm* blowing it?" Fiona

demanded. "Just the other day you said I was working like a pro."

"You are," Woody responded fairly. "And I respect that. But you have to realize that this is a group of high school kids and most of them have absolutely no interest in being professional theater or dance people. Certainly none of them have professional training. You can't expect them to behave like your classmates at Kingsmont."

"I'm not expecting that. I'm just asking them to do their best, that's all. Not to make the play into a big joke. Besides," Fiona added after a pause, "Did you see Phoebe today? She was great. She's been practicing more and trying harder. I can tell. Pushing her has worked," Fiona insisted.

Woody rolled his eyes. "That might be true, Fiona, but the point is, the kids are upset and I thought I should warn you. It will make life easier for everyone." He turned away with a sigh, disappointed that he hadn't gotten through to Fiona at all.

"What's he doing here?" Fiona suddenly gasped aloud.

Woody looked up. Dee and Marc had just walked in with Elise, Tommy, and a couple of Woody's stagehands. Jonathan Preston towered behind Marc.

"Hey, the whole gang's finally turned up!" Woody cheered, rushing over to the crowd's table. Fiona hung back. Since her dream about Jonathan on Monday evening, she felt very uncomfortable around him. One would think in a school as big as Kennedy avoiding someone would be easy. But everywhere Fiona went, Jonathan managed to turn up. He had been at yesterday's rehearsal, and today's, and now he was here.

A burst of applause suddenly went up and Fiona turned around toward the stage, happy to have something divert her attention from Jonathan. The Barn Dance M.C. was making an announcement. He motioned toward an old, white-bearded man wearing a straw cap and denim overalls. When the fiddler started playing a lively tune, the old man launched into some crazy sort of tap dance. Fiona had never seen anything like it! His feet were dancing an Irish jig. It had an intricate rhythm, and his timing was perfect. Fiona watched him, transfixed.

"Bet you've never seen a clog dancer before. He's the gen-u-u-u-uine real thing!"

Jonathan's voice jolted her. "Uh, hi," she said, keeping her eyes on the stage.

"Ever try something like that?" Jonathan asked.

"No. I've done some tap dancing, but nothing like that. What'd you say it was called?" She turned and looked up into Jonathan's eyes.

He was wearing a jaunty straw pork-pie hat, and he had tied a blue-and-white-checked bandanna around his neck. His overalls matched the dancer's and his shirt sleeves and were rolled up. The outfit made him look taller and leaner and cuter than ever. "That guy's Country Will Chester. He's a real hillbilly from back in the Tennessee Hills — one of the most famous clog dancers alive."

Fiona forced herself to look away from Jonathan. With her eyes fixed on Country Will, she said, "I wish I could dance like that."

"I'm sure it wouldn't be hard for someone like you to pick up."

Before Fiona could protest, Jonathan pulled her through the crowd over to the side of the stage. "I learned this dance at boy scout camp once. It goes sort of like this, only faster." Jonathan demonstrated a few steps.

They were simple. It was just the rhythm that was tricky, but Fiona had very fast feet and a perfect sense of timing. In a couple of minutes she had the basic steps down. Then she heard a voice call down from the stage: "Here's a little miss who *sure* can dance up a storm. Mr. Chester here's a bit shy, but I bet ya he'd love to have a partner."

Fiona looked up and her eyes widened in horror. The M.C. was talking into his mike, stretching his hand down toward her's. The crowd began stomping and cheering. Fiona started to back off, then spotted Country Will Chester over the M.C.'s shoulder, inviting her to join him.

"Okay," she heard herself saying. "I'll give it a try." Two strong hands gripped her around the waist and hoisted her up to the stage. From the surge of warmth that rushed through her, Fiona knew the hands were Jonathan's. For a dizzying moment she stood at the edge of the stage, the spotlights blinding her eyes, feeling like she was going to faint. Then Country Will hobbled over to her, gently pulled her hand through his arm, and gave it a friendly squeeze. "Don't be afraid." He grinned toothlessly. "Jist watch me."

The fiddle struck up a tune, and Fiona tried to follow Country Will's dance. Suddenly her feet seemed to take off on their own, and for the first time in her life Fiona Stone — ballerina — was clogging and stomping on the hollow wooden stage with Country Will Chester.

When the dance ended, applause, catcalls, and whistles shook the barn.

Fiona turned around and gave Country Will a huge smile, then hurried to the side of the stage where her eyes sought Jonathan in the crowd.

He was there, waiting with outstretched arms. She hopped down with her hands on his shoulders. For a second he held her aloft, and twirled her around. As he lowered her to the ground, his lips gently brushed her forehead. His lips were incredibly soft and Fiona's heart raced when he murmured, "That was so beautiful. . . ." Fiona studied her feet in confusion. She knew Jonathan wasn't just talking about her dancing.

Then Woody and the crew were gathered around them, pushing and shouting. Jeremy had finally turned up with Diana, and Fiona grinned triumphantly at him. Everyone crowded around her and Fiona giggled nervously, then edged away from Jonathan. She was suddenly embarrassed. They must have seen him kiss her.

"You are the best dancer I've ever seen!" Phoebe cried. "If only I could move like you!"

Fiona suddenly remembered why she was there. "You can," she said briskly. "You just have to work harder." She turned away from Phoebe, and started addressing the cast, "Tonight, every one of you in the play should really be working on trying to learn these square and round dances perfectly. I bet no one's even danced yet." She put her hands on her hips and eyeballed each member of the cast.

"Ugh!" Phoebe moaned audibly. "Why did I open my big mouth?" She flashed Fiona a disgusted look and marched back to the table.

When she was halfway there, Michael grabbed her arm, and pulled her over to a private corner. "Phoebe, calm down." He wrapped his arms around her, and rocked her back and forth.

"You heard her. She keeps picking on me," Phoebe grumbled. "She acts like I'm so dumb. I feel so — so big and clumsy around her." Her voice trembled.

"Phoebe, stop that. You're beautiful, and I love you," Michael assured her with a gentle kiss. He crouched down on the floor and Phoebe crouched down next to him. She lightly rested her head against his shoulder. "It's not you she's picking on. It's everybody." For the first time that week Michael sounded annoyed at Fiona.

Phoebe gave an exaggerated sigh of relief. "I can't believe Ms. Perfect's halo is slipping at last."

"Don't be unfair, Phoebe. I still respect her, but she's driving everyone too hard. You're right about that. She has to learn how to work with people."

"If she doesn't figure it out soon, she's not going to have anyone to work with," Phoebe forecasted with a shake of her braid.

Michael got up and pulled Phoebe to her feet.

"Pheeb," he said, tenderly brushing the stray red curls off her forehead, "Sitting in a dark corner moping over Fiona isn't much fun is it?" Phoebe's worried face relaxed into a warm smile.

"Not as much fun as dancing," she suggested, a playful gleam in her eyes. A raucous square dance was in progress. The caller was commanding everyone to take their partners and do-si-do. Woody, Dee, Marc, and Kim were wreaking havoc in one square, reducing all the other dancers to wild laughter. "Will you dance with me?" Michael asked with an exaggerated bow.

Phoebe pretended to consider his request, then curtsied awkwardly in her overalls, and took his arm. They skipped over to join Jeremy, Diana, Holly, and Bart, just as everyone began swinging their partners.

Phoebe was giggling, and managed to miss the next call. Everyone began their do-si-do, while she was still bowing to Bart who was no longer there. She shrugged her shoulders, and improvised with a couple of skips and hops until she could follow the dance again. Then Phoebe spotted Fiona at the next square — frowning disgustedly at their group.

Woody didn't believe in being angry. He abhorred violence and hadn't punched anyone in the nose since he was ten years old.

But at the moment, he was trying very hard not to punch Fiona Stone. Somehow Woody and Kim had ended up in the same set with Fiona and now she was playing drill sergeant during every dance. Woody was about to hit the ceiling.

"Come on, Woody. Watch those dancers over there — they have the right spirit. Lift your feet up, like this. Kick them behind you. You're playing jaunty Will and Ado Annie's the kind of girl you want to kick up your heels about." No one laughed at Fiona's joke. At the end of the dance, the set broke up. Elise dragged herself over to a corner and flopped down on a bench near one of the stage hands. Woody grabbed Kim's hand and stormed off after Elise. Fiona looked around puzzled. Only Jonathan was left by her side.

"Rehearsal was over around five o'clock," Jonathan reminded her gently.

Fiona rolled her eyes to the ceiling. "Jobs end at five o'clock; schools ends at three; art doesn't have a timetable, Jonathan," she said. "The whole purpose of coming here was to learn the steps, watch the dances. Not to — "

"I know, clown around," Jonathan said. "But don't you think people can learn by having fun?"

"I feel an argument coming on," Fiona said after struggling to contain her temper. She was determined not to fight with Jonathan tonight. Her hand drifted to the spot where he had kissed her. She still felt they were wrong for each other, but the thought made her sad tonight, not angry. If only Jonathan Preston were more directed, more serious. If he could only understand where she was coming from. Fiona felt the silence growing awkward so she told him she was thirsty and

133

Jonathan followed close on her heels, then paid for her soda before she could pull the change out of her skirt pocket.

The M.C. announced the last dance, and as the lights dimmed, a chorus of sighs and protests greeted his announcement. "As you regulars know, the last dance is traditionally a slow waltz. A couple of our experts will demonstrate for the first few measures, then everyone join in. See you next week, partners."

The floor cleared except for an elderly couple who started off the waltz. It was a slow, restrained version Fiona had never seen before. She gazed with rapt attention at the couple, and barely noticed when Jonathan took the soda from her hand. A second later his arm was around her waist and they glided across the dimly lit dance floor. Fiona wanted to protest, but she couldn't. The music had cast a spell on her, so had the dark, and the memory of Jonathan's kiss. She closed her eyes and let herself drift along with him across the room. They held each other close as they danced into the shadows behind the stage. When the music ended, Jonathan tilted her face up and met her lips with his.

# Chapter
## 14

Phoebe slouched down in the chair and stuffed her hands deeper into the pockets of her soft wool pants. She hadn't slept all night and now her head ached. She pressed her fingers against her temples and squeezed her eyes shut tight. The noise in the auditorium was deafening. Phoebe wanted to tune out the whole assembly, or better yet she wanted to go home, crawl into bed and not come out again until *Oklahoma!* was all over. Then she wouldn't have to look at Fiona Stone.

A glum-looking Woody slipped into the seat between Phoebe and Kim. He snapped Phoebe's green plaid suspenders and said, "You look about as good as I feel."

Phoebe pushed her hair off her face and grimaced at Woody. "I look *that* bad?"

Kim leaned across Woody and patted Phoebe's

arm. "If Dr. Holly were here she'd diagnose another case of the Fionas."

"Seems to be an epidemic," Bart said. He was sitting on the other side of Phoebe cramming for an afternoon math exam.

Phoebe looked at Bart gratefully. She had felt too loyal to Woody to say it to anybody, but secretly she was beginning to feel the whole show should be scrapped. Only Woody's incredible energy seemed to keep the production on its feet. Phoebe knew every member of the cast was gritting its teeth and hanging in there, trying to weather Fiona's storminess — only because they felt loyal to Woody. Phoebe loved Woody too much to seriously consider quitting *Oklahoma!*, even though she wanted to after each rehearsal with Fiona.

Sasha spoke up from further down the row. "I heard from Dee yesterday about the trouble the cast was having."

"I didn't think our problems on the set were such big news around the quad," Bart commented.

"Well, news *is* news. And I do have a nose for it," Sasha admitted. "But Pheeb," Sasha said, "Dee also told me how much Fiona likes you. She just wants to put on a good show."

"Spare me," Phoebe said as Chris Austin stepped center stage and pounded a gavel on the podium. "All Fiona believes in is herself, and her dancing pals back at Kingsmont."

Phoebe's voice rang out in the sudden silence that filled the auditorium. Just then, Fiona walked into the room and spotted an empty seat beside

136

Sasha. The conversation down the row suddenly died.

Phoebe shifted uncomfortably in her seat as Sasha said, "Hi, Fiona."

An angry blush flooded Fiona's face. Phoebe had been talking about her. So had Woody and Bart. Every one of them avoided her eyes. She sat up very tall and stared straight ahead, pretending that she hadn't noticed.

Mr. Beman, the principal, finally bellowed some opening remarks into the mike. Fiona leaned back and closed her eyes. She wished that this were a special assembly — a movie or musical performance, where the lights would be turned down. Then she could stop holding back her tears. She had thought the kids in the cast were her friends, especially Phoebe and Woody. But friends didn't talk behind each others' backs.

Fiona was considering sneaking out when she heard Mr. Beman introducing Jonathan Preston. Jonathan was walking across the stage in a soft gray shirt, goofy print tie, baggy wool pants, and his crazy felt hat. He looked more like a stand-up comic than like someone about to address a school assembly.

Fiona blushed, thinking about how wonderful kissing him had felt. She didn't know how she had let it happen. And then she remembered she had agreed to go bowling on Friday night with Jonathan, Jeremy and Diana, and Peter and Monica. How did she let herself get into such impossible situations? She and Jonathan had nothing in common, and she planned to tell him that next time she saw him.

Suddenly something Jonathan was saying caught her ear. Fiona leaned forward to hear him better. He was describing the results of the Holiday Homeless Drive so far. The figures were impressive and so was Jonathan. He talked as naturally in front of two thousand kids as he did with just her or Jeremy. Fiona wondered when in the world he had prepared his talk. Last night he had been out dancing until late and he hadn't mentioned addressing the assembly at all. Fiona couldn't understand. She would have stayed home every night for a week, trying to get her presentation just right.

Fiona listened to Jonathan in amazement. It wasn't just the speech he was giving, it was the fact that in over a month he had raised a thousand dollars for his drive. Plus enough food and clothing contributions to fill the basement of Garfield House. But Fiona couldn't remember him ever talking about all this work. He was always clowning around, or socializing, and having fun.

Jonathan's remark about all work and no play suddenly popped into Fiona's head. He hadn't just been fooling around, he had been trying to tell her something he knew from experience. Fiona squirmed slightly in her seat. She hadn't listened to him. A panicky feeling welled up inside her. She hadn't understood Jonathan at all until just now.

Jonathan ended his talk with an honest appeal.

Fiona felt he was looking directly at her as he said, "The spirit of how we raise this money for the homeless is as important as the act of raising it. Learning to work together for a cause is almost as important as the cause itself."

Fiona slipped out of the auditorium before Jonathan finished his speech. She headed straight for the library, and her favorite hideaway: a little niche on the far wall behind the rows of fiction. There was an empty, hollow feeling in the pit of her stomach, and she needed to spend some time alone to straighten out her thoughts.

She was hurt because of Phoebe and the fact that her friends had been talking about her behind her back. It was Jonathan, however, that she was most upset about. Just as she was starting to see him as a boy she could fall in love with, someone who wasn't so wrong for her after all, she realized how badly she'd been treating him. She had been so caught up with her work on the play, as Jonathan pointed out, that she hadn't stopped for a minute to consider how he felt about her. She wouldn't blame him if he didn't show up to take her bowling on Friday night. Last night, after the dance, she hadn't even said good-bye.

# *Chapter*
# *15*

Jeremy bent low, took a couple of quick steps forward, swung his right arm back, and hurled his bowling ball as hard as he could. It bounced and clattered right into the gutter. Even after it vanished at the far end of the lane, Jeremy continued to watch the bowling pins, expecting them somehow to all fall down. He shook his head and turned around.

Peter Lacey booed. His powerful voice echoed throughout Rose Hill Lanes. "Stone, that was the pits!"

Jeremy grinned foolishly and stuffed his hands in his sweater pockets. "Does that mean I lose?"

"No." Diana stood up and tucked her red checked shirt into the top of her jeans. As she reached for her ball she said, "It means *we* lose." She narrowed her dark eyes and feigned a mean, hard look. He planted an apologetic kiss on the top of her nose and she laughed. "You're impossible. Watch this," she said softly, then tossed her silver-blonde hair over her shoulders and marched up to the foot of the lane. She bit her lip in concentration, then broke into her stride. Her ball sailed straight down the center of the lane, then curved slightly for a perfect strike.

Everyone cheered but Jeremy. Diana looked around and planted her hands on her hips. Jeremy hadn't been watching. He was staring up at the Pepsi-Cola clock suspended over the refreshment stand. It was seven-forty. "I wonder where Jonathan and Fiona are." Jonathan had told Jeremy he'd pick Fiona up after rehearsal. They were supposed to meet at the bowling alley at six-thirty.

"Quit worrying, Stone. They're probably the same place they were at six . . . and at seven . . ." Peter said with a laugh.

Jeremy looked at him blankly. "But Fiona's not like this. She promised she'd come here tonight. She's always on time, and she never breaks promises."

Diana reached for Jeremy's hand and pulled him down beside her on the seat. "It's what you wanted, isn't it?" she reminded him. "I think you should relax a bit about Fiona."

Monica readily assented. "I'm sure she's capable of taking care of herself. Woody and the rest of the *Oklahoma!* cast expected a shy, quiet dance director when Ms. Everson picked Fiona. I hear she's been a regular drill sergeant running those rehearsals."

"You're wrong, Monica. You don't know Fiona

at all. She couldn't be like that if she tried. She's way too sweet," Jeremy insisted.

"Sweet?" Diana gulped, then forced herself not to continue. To spare Jeremy's feelings, she hadn't repeated Bart's stories about working with Fiona. He had said today's rehearsal had been the worst yet. He'd even muttered something to her about everyone quitting the show. Now that Monica had brought the subject up, Diana saw the opening she had been waiting for. Maybe, just maybe, Jeremy could get through to his sister . . . if someone could get to Jeremy before it was too late. "To tell you the truth, Bart said she's been anything but sweet these days. I've heard the cast is really up in arms."

"The Kennedy Players just aren't used to working hard," Jeremy began, pacing the floor in front of the others. "Fiona works hard, and she is a bit stubborn, but she's a professional and acts like one. Phoebe, and Woody — the whole lot of them aren't used to it. So they complain a lot. That's not such a big deal."

"But it is," Peter broke in. He met Jeremy's eyes squarely. "It's a very big deal, Stone. This is a community fund-raising event, not just any old school play. If this show falls through, your sister will be to blame."

Jeremy's mouth fell open. "My sister's doing a great job with this show. Have you seen the rehearsals? You don't know what you're talking about."

Peter took a deep breath and spoke in a controlled voice. "I haven't been to the rehearsals.

142

But I've been spending enough time with Woody, Bart, and Phoebe around school and in the sub shop to hear that things aren't going too well. I don't know where you've been that you haven't noticed, but you can get through to her. She is your sister."

"That's right, Lacey," Jeremy snapped. "She is my sister, and I know her better than any of you. I think it's pretty unfair of Woody, Phoebe, and everyone else to blame problems with the show on Fiona. She's just trying to do the best job she can. If they can't take the pressure, that's their problem," Jeremy concluded. "I've had enough bowling for tonight," he said, reaching for his jacket. "Ready to go, Diana?"

She got up slowly with a sigh. "You tried," she whispered to Monica and Peter.

"We all tried. But when it comes to his sister, he's really blind," Monica said. She and Peter stood up and followed Diana out to the parking lot.

Fiona took one deep breath after another trying to ease the tightness in her chest. She sat huddled in the center of the stage, her arms wrapped around her knees. The stage lights were down, the old chapel was drafty. The light had faded from the circular window above the choir loft. It was already dark outside and rehearsal had broken up hours ago — but Fiona had lost track of the time. She was desperately trying to figure out how to salvage the show. Monday was dress rehearsal and the musical was still in tatters.

Not in that scary way that you knew would end when all the bits and pieces snapped together at the last minute. Fiona had a feeling things were just going to get worse.

Her first impulse was to blame the cast's bad attitude on Phoebe Hall. But, it wasn't just Phoebe who had been uncooperative. Overnight Bart had developed a severe case of two left feet. Elise forgot all the steps to the final production number and today even Woody had seemed irritable. Usually he prodded the players into at least trying to please Fiona. Today, he just sulked his way around the set, barking orders at everyone.

Fiona cupped her chin in her hands and stared into the darkened auditorium. But she couldn't blame Woody or Phoebe for the problems the cast was having. She could only blame herself. If she could only think clearly, she could figure out where she was going wrong. But Fiona couldn't think now. She felt so hurt, so powerless, so out-of-control — the way she had felt when she had flubbed the audition for the National Ballet. Here she was, back on stage, failing again. Fiona slammed her hand down hard on the floorboards and shook her head miserably. When would she ever learn? She should have learned her lesson that horrible day on the stage back in England. She had given her best, and it wasn't enough. Three thousand miles away, a couple of months later, she was replaying the same scene all over again.

"I hate being stood up!" A voice suddenly echoed through the theater.

Fiona looked up. Beneath the safety lights she could barely make out his face. But there was no mistaking the tall figure in the aisle. "Jonathan!" she exclaimed joyfully. For the first time since she'd met him she was really glad to see him. The dark cold theater suddenly seemed to light up. The hollow feeling inside of her receded. She jumped up and started down the stairs clutching her dance bag, and then she remembered. "Bowling!" Her hand dropped limply to her side. "Oh, Jonathan, I forgot."

"Better late than never," Jonathan said evenly. He gestured toward the door. Fiona walked quickly down the aisle after him. Jonathan turned up the collar of his jacket, and as he stood beneath the lamplight, Fiona wondered why he had gotten so dressed up just to go bowling. Watching him, tall and very handsome in his stylishly baggy suit and narrow tie, Fiona suddenly felt tongue-tied.

"Big Pink's waiting," he said and ushered her across the quad toward the car. Fiona followed without a word of protest, skirting the puddles. She couldn't believe she had forgotten about their bowling date, but she had blanked out on everything after the rehearsal. She looked over at Jonathan as they pulled out onto the dark highway.

She wanted to reach across the seat and touch his arm, tell him how glad she was he had shown up. She wished they were going somewhere alone. She certainly wasn't in the mood for a triple date at Rose Hill Lanes. She wanted to tell Jonathan exactly what she had felt during yesterday's assembly. Watching him talk she felt like she had seen him for the first time. He was no longer just a good-looking, tall, gray-eyed boy who took her on a date because her brother had asked him to. He was a person she was beginning to really like. Now feeling the way she had when she kissed him was beginning to make more sense. Maybe they weren't from such different planets after all.

# Chapter
# 16

"Jonathan—" she cried out suddenly. "Where are we going?"

Jonathan had just driven clear down Rosemont, past the huge neon bowling pin that flashed in alternate green and red lights: ROSE HILL LANES. He turned right, onto the Beltway.

"Not bowling," he answered. "I guess we owe your brother an apology for tonight."

Fiona gaped at him. She was about to demand that he take her home, but one look at the bumper-to-bumper traffic and she decided it was safer not to argue. She hadn't wanted to go bowling anyway.

Five minutes later, Jonathan pulled into the underground parking garage at the Kennedy Center. Fiona's eyes widened. "We're going here?" she exclaimed, wondering what was playing. She looked down at her baggy legwarmers, then over at Jonathan. "I'm not dressed for a place like this."

"Sorry, Fiona. I never had a chance to tell you. I went to the theater yesterday after practice but you were busy and I had to run. I didn't feel like telling Jeremy about this," he added. "I guess they're all at Rose Hill Lanes wondering what happened to us by now."

Fiona giggled nervously. She could imagine exactly what her brother was thinking — what he was hoping for all along was finally happening. She was going out with Jonathan without Jeremy having planned it. Then Jonathan continued. "If you hadn't stood me up, we would have had time for you to change. Besides," he added, a twinkle in his eyes, "You look fine, Fiona."

Fiona self-consciously smoothed her hair, pleased by his compliment. Before he could open her door, she climbed out of the car. They headed for the nearest elevator bank, with Fiona walking a little ahead of him. Now and then he'd touch her arm or shoulder lightly, guiding her through the well-dressed crowd. Each touch sent off a shiver of electric sparks. She had a crazy desire to turn around and reach up and kiss him, right in the middle of all these people, but she was afraid. Not of what people would think, but of Jonathan. What if he didn't want to kiss her back? What if Wednesday night had been an accident, a mistake — something he regretted?

When the elevator door opened, she saw a poster on the back wall. American Ballet Theatre. Fiona whirled around. "Jonathan, we're going to the *ballet*?" she practically shrieked. Jonathan steered her into the packed elevator. "I thought you'd prefer it to bowling," he said softly, taking her hand. Fiona's eyes filled with tears. She sniffed them back quietly. There was so much she suddenly wanted to say! But she couldn't talk to him here — there wasn't even enough room to turn around and look at him. Instead, she kept her eyes on the elevator door and shyly squeezed his hand.

The lights went down a second after they reached their seats. Jonathan helped Fiona off with her jacket during the overture to the first short ballet, his hand lingering on her shoulder a minute longer than necessary. Then the curtain went up and she hadn't even had a chance to see the program. *Rodeo!* she gasped, quickly covering her mouth with her hand. A second later she forgot about Jonathan, about being in an audience, about today's dismal rehearsal. The De Mille choreography was so perfect, so vibrant, so evocative of the Wild West. Fiona's soul was soon filled with the music and she danced every step of the ballet in her mind. At the end, the curtain came down, the lights went up, and Fiona was still staring at the empty stage.

"Much better than bowling," Jonathan said, watching Fiona's face. Her eyes shone, and her cheeks were pink, as if she really had been down there dancing under the hot lights.

They shared a Coke during intermission, and wandered around the spacious theater lobby. Suddenly, Fiona couldn't stop talking about dance. She told Jonathan what it felt like under

149

the lights, with sweat pouring down your face, muscles straining, having to smile even though your ankle was about to give out, your tutu was torn, and your partner had just messed up on the choreography.

The theater lights blinked twice and they hurried back to their seats. This time when the curtain went up, Fiona's heart stopped. The setting was familiar: Juliet's bedroom at dawn, Romeo at the window. It was Fiona's favorite ballet — one she would be dancing in a year or two had she made it into the National Ballet. The music started softly, with a strain of violins. Juliet woke up and ran to Romeo by the window. He wrapped her in his cloak and the dance began. Fiona had rehearsed this *pas de deux* a hundred times — she knew every step. As she watched, she pictured herself on stage as Juliet, and suddenly her heart was breaking. She jumped up and pushed her way past Jonathan, down the row of annoyed spectators, out into the aisle. She ran up the stairs, and into the hall. As the black auditorium door swung shut behind her, she burst into tears.

Jonathan appeared behind her, her coat and bag in his hands. He motioned away an approaching usher, and firmly took Fiona's elbow, guiding her through the empty upstairs lobby. Tears streamed down Fiona's face and she held her hands over her ears to block out the music that slipped under the closed doors of the auditorium.

Jonathan led her to a corner where he gathered her in his arms and drew her down beside him on the carpeted stairs. Fiona pressed her face against his chest and sobbed.

"It's all right, Fiona," Jonathan murmured tenderly. "Let it out. All this time you've been hurting so much — and I didn't know." He sounded so gentle, as if he could really feel the same hurt she felt. His large warm hand smoothed her back. Fiona leaned into his touch and slowly the pain inside her began to subside.

"Oh, Jonathan," she whispered through her tears. "I'm so sorry. Crying like this — I made such a scene — " She pulled away slightly, keeping her face away from his. She rubbed her cheeks with her hand. Her mascara had run, her skin was probably all blotchy. She must look a mess. She didn't want Jonathan to see her like this.

He put his finger under her chin, and tilted her face toward his. "You're even beautiful when you cry," he said, producing a silly polka dot handkerchief from his breast pocket. "Considering you're a professional performer, you didn't make *that* much of a scene." He gently dabbed the tears from her cheeks. She took the handkerchief from him and blew her nose, sniffed some more, then shook her head. "I didn't know — I didn't know seeing it would affect me so much." Her voice came out all creaky and small.

"I'm sorry you're not having a good time," Jonathan said after a pause.

Fiona caught her breath. "Oh, no. I'm glad we came. Really, I am — it's been so long since I've seen real dancing. I had begun to forget." She closed her eyes. When she began to speak again,

151

it was with great effort. "I — didn't think watching other people dance the things I used to dance would make me feel like this." She wound and unwound the handkerchief in her hand, then rubbed her forehead. Her head was suddenly pounding. "Watching them just now, I felt as if — as if I were dancing with them."

"You used to dance this — *Romeo and Juliet*?" Jonathan's voice held a mixture of surprise and pain. "Oh, I shouldn't have brought you here. I didn't know. But it sounded so romantic." His eyes held hers for a long deep second.

Suddenly Fiona had to talk. She had to let it all out: the shapeless, awful feelings she'd had for weeks now; her decision to quit ballet. Her head had told her to stop, but her body couldn't listen. It kept right on dancing. When she looked up at Jonathan, her eyes were filled with tears. "I can't face it. I can't face not dancing again, and yet I can't face dancing, either. It all feels so crazy. I just hurt so much. You can't imagine how humiliating it was not succeeding at something I'd been working toward my whole life." She buried her head in her arms.

Jonathan leaned his cheeks against her shaking shoulders and stroked her arms with his hands. When her tears subsided, Jonathan sat up. He massaged the back of Fiona's neck as she blew her nose.

"I don't know exactly how you feel," Jonathan admitted, wishing with all his heart he could. "I'm not a dancer. But I watched you dancing at The Barn Dance the other night, and I saw you come alive. Fiona, you *are* a dancer. You can't choose one way or the other."

Fiona stared at him. "I never thought of it like that. Until I danced again at the *Oklahoma!* try-outs, and at The Barn Dance, I didn't *feel* alive." Fiona was filled with wonder. How did Jonathan know that about her? "But it's over now. Even the show's going badly. I don't think I'm meant to make it in the dance world."

"Fiona," Jonathan said. "I saw how you push those kids in *Oklahoma!* You're a pretty strong-willed person. If you *want* to dance again, you'll do it — against all odds." He took her by the shoulders and forced her to face him. He stared straight into her eyes and said, "Just because you flubbed one audition, it doesn't end your career. You've got to get up, brush off the dust, and move on. You'll fail lots of times but you'll get up lots of times, too. It's like that." Fiona was locked into his intense gaze. Suddenly, she knew he was right.

"I think you should try out for a company here in D.C.," Jonathan suggested cautiously. "There are lots of places to study dance here. You were born to dance, Fiona, and if you don't, you're going to become a very unhappy person. You're too strong-minded to sit back and give up on what you want." He considered his next words carefully. "I think if you were doing what you loved — ballet — even in a classroom — everything else you do would go more smoothly. The play would go better. You wouldn't drive everyone around you so hard."

"I'm not driving everyone too hard," Fiona

153

countered instantly, recalling today's rehearsal. "I don't ask anyone to do what I wouldn't."

Jonathan didn't back down. "Yes, you do. You're asking these kids who don't care about dancing to give you their hearts and souls. If you don't at least try to keep dancing ballet, you're not giving your best."

Jonathan's words pierced Fiona. The pressure behind her eyes built up, and a few tears spilled out before she said, "So what can I do?"

"Try out for a company here," Jonathan repeated.

"I haven't had a class for weeks," Fiona moaned. She felt Jonathan had opened a door and pushed her through . . . and now he was blocking the way back. She couldn't hide in her room anymore. She had to at least try to dance again. She couldn't picture a future without dancing. She'd have to try it again, even though she knew her chances of getting into an American company at this point were slim. "I need to find a professional-level class here. I guess that's the first step. The Academy of Ballet Arts in Georgetown holds open auditions for professional classes Tuesday mornings. I guess I should try that," Fiona said nervously.

The crowd began filing out of the auditorium. Fiona and Jonathan scrambled to their feet as the audience made for the elevator banks. Jonathan guided Fiona toward the deserted back stairs. They started down hand in hand. On the first landing Jonathan stopped.

"Will you promise me that?"

She looked up into Jonathan's concerned eyes. He really cared about her. Fiona's heart thrilled watching him look at her like that. Then she remembered what he wanted to hear.

It took all her courage but she finally whispered, "I promise. Tuesday morning I'll try out. And if it doesn't work, well, I'll try somewhere else." Fiona's voice caught on the last few words. In her whole life, she had never broken a promise. And she wouldn't now.

Jonathan lowered his face toward hers. He traced the outline of her delicate face with his fingers. "You are so beautiful," he whispered, kissing the tears from her face. Fiona lifted her mouth toward his. He kissed her gently, the way he had kissed her during their last dance the other night. Her arms tightened around his neck. She nuzzled his ear, and ran her fingers through his thick hair. Then her lips found his again. After a moment, she pulled away to catch her breath.

Jonathan gazed at her, a small smile on his mouth. He put one hand on each side of her shoulders and pressed her against the wall of the stairwell. "You look so delicate, but you're so strong. I love you, Fiona," he said, and kissed her again, this time more passionately, until Fiona no longer felt the damp concrete pressing through her thin jacket, or heard the sound of the cars in the garage below.

# *Chapter* *17*

Fiona hurried into the prop room of the Little Theater and reminded herself this was dress rehearsal, the last chance before the countdown to showtime began. Not that she needed much reminding. Her stomach was churning and she was scared to death, but her step was strong and confident as she headed across the floor to the girls' costume rack. She *knew* she was back in control again. The show wouldn't fail: Fiona was sure of that now. Her talk with Jonathan on Friday had bolstered her confidence. She was positive that with just a bit more determination, she could whip the cast into shape and get this musical back on track. She decided to look at Friday's disastrous rehearsal as just one more time she had tripped and fallen. Now she'd get back up, dust herself off, and start all over again this afternoon. It wasn't too late.

The commotion backstage was at fever pitch. Fiona wove her way through the cast and crew. For a second, she wondered why everyone looked so tense and glum as they scooted from one side of the room to the other, yelling at Henry and Janie about parts of their costumes. Fiona got a funny feeling in the pit of her stomach, then willed it away. Today was not going to be a disaster — she wasn't going to let it happen.

Woody was in a corner, half in costume. The tails of his cowboy shirt flapped over his jeans as he argued with Bart and a couple of other guys dressed in cow punch gear. Bart sat on a bare stump morosely strumming minor chords on his guitar. Woody shook him by the shoulders and Bart's handsome face broke into a slow grin. Fiona heard him say in his slow Western drawl, "For you, partner, I'll give it one last try. Remember, though, this is the showdown."

Fiona wondered absent-mindedly what they were talking about as she reached for her own costume. She took it into the girls' dressing room just as Phoebe came out in the pretty blue gingham dress she wore in the first act. Fiona smiled. "You look great, Phoebe." Without thanking or even acknowledging Fiona, Phoebe marched right past her out the door.

Fiona arched her eyebrows and slammed the dressing room door behind Phoebe. She peeled off her clothes, pulled on her tights and slipped the white gauzy dress for the dream sequence over her head. It fit perfectly. Fiona stretched her arms up and gracefully did some side bends. The dress felt fine. She swirled once in the narrow room. The skirt moved perfectly. She studied her reflection in the mirror, then sank down on the chair in front of the dressing table and tried to organize her thoughts, concentrate on which routines needed the most work, and which costumes might cause the most problems. Fiona couldn't focus on any one thing. Thinking about anything logically had been impossible ever since Friday. After Jonathan had kissed her and told her he loved her, Fiona's mind had scarcely been on the problems with *Oklahoma!*

She never dreamed falling in love would feel like this. She had barely made it through her classes today. Every time Fiona thought of Jonathan she got a delicious, warm feeling. She looked for him everywhere, even though she knew she seldom saw him during the school day. Their schedules were too different.

It wasn't just Jonathan that had her muddled. It was that dumb promise she had made. Whatever had possessed her to promise she would try out for the Ballet Arts tomorrow before school?

Fiona pressed her palms to her eyes and got up. She couldn't worry about tomorrow's tryout now. At the moment, she had work to do. Today's rehearsal was just as crucial for Fiona's future. She hadn't confided in Jonathan about how terribly the show had been going. Admitting how scared she was about the show failing would have made it all seem too real. She pulled on her ballet slippers and went off to check the lights. Last time she looked, Woody's assistant had put on all the wrong gels.

"Fiona." Dee hurried across the crowded stage with a camera in her hand. "You look super!" she complimented, then lowered her voice. "Jonathan's here. He's with Jeremy in the back row." Last night Fiona had told Dee about their night at the ballet. Fiona smiled at Dee, then with a friendly shove, pushed her toward the wings. "Cast only, Deirdre Patterson. Besides, aren't you supposed to be taking pictures?" Fiona scolded. "Oh, Dee, I can't even let myself *think* of Jonathan now. Wish me luck," she whispered, her voice trembling.

Dee gave her a quick hug, then left the stage. Fiona asked one of the stage hands to close the curtain, then she searched for Woody. It was up to him to start the rehearsal. He wasn't in the wings or backstage. Fiona poked her head out of the curtain. Woody was standing in the orchestra pit, talking to Michael. Michael's face was screwed up with worry.

"Woody?" Fiona cried, stepping up to the lights and tapping her foot impatiently. "What's happening? Aren't we going to start? We don't want to be here all night."

"Whenever *you're* ready, *we* begin," Woody said sharply. His voice had an edge to it. Fiona had never heard Woody talk like that before. She swallowed hard. Rehearsal hadn't even started yet and she was sure something was about to go terribly wrong.

Woody waved at Michael, then leaped up on the stage, his spurs jangling, and the taps on the bottom of his boots clicking as he stepped into the wings.

Fiona glared at Woody, then marched to the side of the stage and clapped her hands. "Places, everyone," she shouted. Then she motioned for Michael to play the last few bars of the overture. Two measures off cue, the curtain jerked up. Fiona made a mental note to go over the score yet one more time with the stage crew.

Bart's opening song went well. The first few scenes were passable though Phoebe looked as if her heart really wasn't in the role. Fiona tried to ignore it but she couldn't ignore Phoebe's screw-up in the girls' big dance number. She was supposed to dance with the chorus, then step aside as Fiona took over the dancing lead. After a week of intensive rehearsals Phoebe had completely forgotten the steps.

"Stop the music!" Fiona suddenly cried. She dropped out of her position behind Phoebe and strode angrily center stage. "What's the matter with you?" she said to Phoebe. "You look limp as a rag, and you were supposed to move to the left just now, not the right. It's one-two-three hop, step, turn." Fiona demonstrated, then took a deep breath. "Let's take the whole number from the top."

Phoebe gritted her teeth, but obediently went back to her position and pretended to look out at her boyfriend Curly laughing with another girl.

This time as she started singing "Many a New Day," her voice quavered. Fiona was pretty tone deaf but Phoebe was singing so flat even she noticed it. Fiona stood still, waiting for Woody to stop Phoebe. He didn't. Out of the corner of her eye she spotted him in the wings, looking edgy and upset. Woody wasn't even paying attention. He certainly wasn't going to say anything to Phoebe about her singing.

Fiona cursed under her breath, and shouted to Michael to stop playing. "You were flat," she said to Phoebe. Phoebe glared at her, then tossed her red braid over her shoulder, and stamped back to the window to start the scene again. This time when the dance started, Phoebe forgot to hop before she turned, and collided with Elise.

Fiona cursed out loud this time. "Phoebe Hall, get your act together," she yelled. "The show opens in two days, and you're falling apart. Now start again. We'll do it until it's right."

"Forget it!" Phoebe suddenly burst out, her huge green eyes filled with fire. She planted her hands on her hips and glared at Fiona. Fiona shook her head in disbelief. What had she ever done to Phoebe Hall? First Phoebe had gossiped about her and now this, defying her in front of the whole cast. Fiona forced down a rising tide of panic.

"I've had it with you, Fiona. I'm tired of you picking on me and I'm tired of being treated like an idiot. Just because I'm not one of your professional dancer friends from Kingsmont doesn't mean you can scream and yell at me all the time.

Why don't you go back to England, where you can surround yourself with real pros from Kingsmont? Until you came along, this show was fun. I've had it. I'm quitting." With that, Phoebe ran right off the stage.

For a second, no one moved.

Fiona stood dumbfounded. She swallowed back the lump in her throat and turned to Woody.

"Woody," Fiona pleaded, "Do something."

"*Do* something?" He shook his head. "It's too late, Fiona. I tried to do something last week. You wouldn't listen. You've been driving the entire cast like slaves, and I'm sick of it. Everyone is. A high school play is supposed to be fun. I don't know what you're trying to prove, but no one around here seems able to please you. I guess you'll just have to find some real pros to give you what you need, not the kids at Kennedy High." Woody's voice was steady and very cool as he said, "I won't help, Fiona. I can't. You see, I'm quitting, too. This is *your* show now." He stormed out into the wings to join Phoebe. Fiona stood in stunned silence as Bart, Elise, Tommy, and the rest of the cast filed out after him.

She closed her eyes and pressed her hands to her temples. This was a nightmare. When she opened her eyes, she would wake up and Phoebe would be there, ready to start her dance again.

She forced herself to open her eyes, but the stage was still deserted. Fiona looked off into the wings. Everyone was gone. A strangled sob rose to her lips. Then she remembered the kids in the audience.

She turned around slowly, instinctively seeking Jonathan. She could make out his shadow in the glare of the lights, towering in the side aisle, facing the stage. Fiona raised her hand to her face and shaded her eyes. Jeremy and Dee were standing by the side door. She wanted so badly to fly down the steps of the stage into Jonathan's arms. He had known so much on Friday. Jonathan understood people so well. Maybe he could fix up this mess, find Woody, Phoebe, explain she was only trying to make the show work because she was miserably afraid of failing. But as Fiona's eyes adjusted to the light, she could see his expression. Her heart caught in her throat and she stood rooted to the spot. Disappointment, pain, and anger were on his face. He shook his head and turned away, then went down the aisle and out the door.

Fiona sank to the floor and broke down. "What am I going to do?" she wailed, burying her face in her arms. "Everyone walked out on me. Everything I touch goes wrong."

Then Jeremy was suddenly by her side. He crouched down beside her, and awkwardly patted her head. Dee scrambled up on stage and knelt down on her other side.

"That's not true, Fiona. You just made a mistake. You aren't used to working with these kids. They aren't dancers like you and your old friends, that's all," Dee said.

Fiona shook her head, and lifted her tear-streaked face toward them. "I don't understand. I tried to do my best. It all backfired. What do I do now?" She looked from Dee to Jeremy.

"I don't know," Jeremy said. "But crying won't help." He stood up and fiddled with his camera. "Fiona, you shouldn't have said those things to Phoebe."

"She was messing up. I was only trying to get her back on track."

"You were too hard on her." Jeremy stepped back. "I should have listened to Peter and Monica the other night. They warned me this would happen."

Fiona rubbed her arm across her nose. "I wasn't too hard on her. Phoebe just won't work hard enough unless I push her." Fiona glared at her brother. "But there's no point talking to you. You've never understood me, and you never will. You're the last person in the world who could realize what's going on now."

Jeremy gasped. He felt as if his sister had just slapped him in the face. Jeremy took a deep breath and started to say something, then thought better of it. With Fiona's bitter words still ringing in his ears, he turned and left the theater.

Dee watched Jeremy walk away, his shoulders sagging. He loved his sister and she had really hurt him. Dee looked down at the sobbing figure of her friend. How had things ever gotten this bad? Fiona was wrong to have treated Phoebe and Jeremy that way, but she was also wrong to think she had failed again. "Poor Fiona," Dee murmured, stroking Fiona's tangled hair. "It's a mess, isn't it? But you haven't blown it, you know."

Fiona sat up and gave a disgusted groan. "Come off it, Dee. It's over." She pulled some tissues out of her dance bag. "Everything's over."

"No, it isn't. It's just begun," Dee said firmly. She forced Fiona to face her. "You have a choice. You can walk away from this, and blame yourself and everyone else in sight for the show falling apart. Or you can call the cast back tomorrow, and apologize."

"Apologize?" Fiona's cheeks flushed angrily. "Are you crazy?" She pulled her arm away from Dee's hand. "How can I face any of those guys? I never want to see them again."

"But, Fiona," Dee pleaded.

Fiona didn't want to talk about it any more. Everything was ruined. There was nothing more to say. "I just want to be alone for a while. Please go." Dee walked off the stage and when she got to the aisle, Fiona broke down in tears again.

# *Chapter*
# *18*

On Tuesday morning, Fiona stood at the foot of the stairs leading to the Academy of Ballet Arts. Strains of Chopin drifted down the stairwell. She put one foot on the bottom step, then hesitated. "What am I doing here?" she asked herself, already knowing the answer. She had told Jonathan she would come, and Fiona always kept her promises. But Fiona wondered if Friday night's promise really meant anything now. Nothing else that had happened Friday between them seemed to. During the disastrous dress rehearsal yesterday, Jonathan, along with the others, had deserted her. Fiona could hardly bear the humiliation of the cast walking out. But she could never stand the pain of Jonathan abandoning her, just when she needed him so much to hold her and tell her everything would work out.

Fiona sank down on the stairs and propped her

elbows on her dance bag. Suddenly the music coming from the dance studio got to her, and Fiona jumped up. She angrily wiped the tears from her eyes. Just because all her hard work on a dumb musical hadn't panned out didn't mean she didn't have what it took to dance — to really dance. Fiona yanked a tissue out of her jacket pocket and blew her nose. She combed her fingers through her hair, shouldered her dance bag, and stormed up the steps to the Academy of Ballet Arts, two at a time.

An hour later Fiona flew down the old wooden steps. "I did it!" she whooped to nobody in particular. As she burst out of the blue painted door into the sunlight, she did a little pirouette, and clapped her hands. Next Monday, as soon as she could fix up her schedule with the guidance counselor, she'd be taking professional dance classes again. She had sailed through her audition.

Fiona started toward the bus stop. A long pink convertible was parked right in front of the bus shelter.

"Jonathan!" she shrieked and started running toward him. "I did it. I got in!" Just before she reached him, she skidded to a halt. Jonathan wasn't smiling. And then Fiona remembered she never wanted to talk to Jonathan Preston again.

"It went well?" he said dryly, opening the car door.

Fiona glared at him and started to walk by. She wasn't about to get into a car with him.

"You'll be late for school."

Fiona turned around. "What are *you* doing here?"

Jonathan looked up and down the street. "It's a public sidewalk." Then he took a deep breath and cleared his throat. "I'm here to give you a ride. I wanted to see how you did, but mostly I wanted to see if you'd show up, if you *really* keep your promises."

"Well, I do."

"Good," Jonathan said. "Because you've got another promise to keep."

Fiona's eyes narrowed. "I only remember making one promise Friday."

"Friday?" Jonathan never took his eyes from her face. "I'm not talking about Friday. I'm talking about the promise you made a couple of weeks ago to choreograph and co-direct a show. You let everyone down yesterday at rehearsal. What do you intend to do about it?"

"None of your business," Fiona replied instantly. "What I decide to do about the show from here on in doesn't concern you. Just like it didn't concern you Friday. I noticed you walked out pretty fast when the sparks started flying."

"I didn't walk out!" he retorted angrily. "I went to find Woody and Ms. Everson. That show *has* to be salvaged. The tickets are sold and the money is already pledged to the Homeless Drive." He punched the palm of one hand with his fist. "Trite as it sounds, the show must go on. And it's your responsibility to see that it does. Your job is to work with the cast members, not against them."

Fiona let his words sink in. She swallowed

hard, then looked up into his clear gray eyes. "Oh, Jonathan, what am I going to do?" she asked, knowing he was right. She couldn't fight the truth. She hadn't worked *with* the cast at all. She had tried to make them into something they couldn't possibly be: professional dancers.

Jonathan's shoulders relaxed. He opened the car door. As Fiona climbed in, he said, "The cast has agreed to meet at three today. If you apologize — and prove to those kids how human you really are, maybe the show will go on."

Fiona twirled and untwirled the strap of her bag. "I'll do it, Jonathan."

"I knew you would," he said softly. Keeping his eyes on the road, he gave her hand a squeeze.

But he didn't kiss her, or tell her he loved her. By the time they got back to school, Fiona's heart was aching. She felt pretty sure she could salvage the show. But not her romance with Jonathan.

# Chapter
# *19*

At the stroke of three, Fiona walked into the Little Theater through the back door. She couldn't face walking down the long aisle into the silence she knew awaited her.

As she passed through the prop room, she noticed the lights were on in the house. There was the buzz of conversation, but none of the usual laughter that preceded rehearsals. Fiona headed into the wings. She stopped a second and wished with all her might that Jonathan would be there, in the back of the audience, watching and cheering her on. He wouldn't be, though. He had said something about a student council meeting over in the gym.

Fiona straightened her shoulders, stood very tall, and walked slowly and deliberately onto the stage. The buzz in the theater died down. When she reached center stage, she turned and faced the audience. The whole cast was there. Fiona's mouth went dry and in an instant of panic, she thought she was about to faint. When she regained her composure, Fiona cleared her throat and began.

"I guess we all know why we're here." She focused her eyes on the red light above the exit door. "Yesterday was a pretty bad scene." Then she shook her head. She knew she sounded all wrong, all hard, like she was about to blame everyone else for what had happened. She took a deep breath and forced herself to look at the audience. Phoebe, Woody, and Michael were in the front row. Elise and Bart were sitting a little further back. Everyone looked so sad, so defeated. Just a week ago they were the craziest group of kids Fiona had ever met. She was responsible for making them look so miserable. "Oh, boy," she whispered, then blurted out, "I'm sorry. I'm so sorry. I didn't mean to make such a mess of things." She stepped over the footlights, and crouched down at the edge of the stage. "I didn't mean to hurt you." She was speaking to everybody, but her eyes looked straight at Phoebe's. "I like you all so much. I never worked with a bunch of people like you before. I guess I got carried away. If you'll give me another chance, I would like to try again. I want to work *with* you this time, to make this show go on."

There was a brief, awkward pause, then suddenly Phoebe was up on the stage. She reached for Fiona's hand and pulled her to her feet. "I'm sorry, too." Phoebe's clear musical voice rang out over the auditorium. "I didn't mean to blow up at you. I just felt dumped on and hurt." She looked at Fiona and grinned foolishly. "And maybe I was a little jealous. I'm really not a very good dancer."

Phoebe threw her arms around Fiona and the two girls hugged each other fiercely. Suddenly Woody bounded up on stage, and the whole crew followed him. Everyone began hugging and kissing. Woody finally clapped his hands.

"Hey, when's rehearsal supposed to begin?" he yelled, then looked at Fiona.

"Whenever you say, Woody. After all, you're the director," Fiona said. Woody gave her a grateful look, then mugged a serious face. "And it's about time I started to act like one." He bellowed instructions to the cast. "In ten minutes I want you all back here, in costume. Dress rehearsal is about to begin." Woody gave his suspenders a big snap, and winked at Fiona. Fiona had never learned how to wink, but she screwed up her face and more or less managed a lopsided squint.

"We're going to pull this show off!" Michael cheered. Rehearsal had broken up and it was too late for a gathering at the sub shop. Fiona, for once, felt sad there'd be no post-rehearsal celebration. Today especially she wanted to hang out with the crowd, the crowd that had suddenly turned into a group of very good friends, people she could laugh and cry and make mistakes with. For the first time since she had arrived in Rose

Hill, she didn't feel like an outsider.

"Fiona," Jeremy called across the parking lot. "I thought you might need a ride," he said, walking toward the little group.

Fiona had avoided Jeremy since the scene in the theater yesterday afternoon.

"I think we need to talk. How about dinner on your brother?" he offered.

Fiona smiled. "I *am* starved. I could go for some pizza."


"Remind me next time I'm broke," Jeremy quipped a half hour later, "not to volunteer to feed a hungry dancer. You practically out-ate Ted Mason."

Fiona laughed. Ted's appetite was legendary on campus. It had been weeks since she'd felt so comfortable around Jeremy. Fiona sat back in her seat and patted her slim stomach. "That just about does it," she said.

Jeremy leaned his elbows on the table. "I wanted to apologize about yesterday. I was a bit rough on you."

"Apology accepted — but not for yesterday. What you said was right, you know," she admitted with a sigh. "I see that now."

"I must say I never expected the show to get back on its feet. How'd you do it? It looked pretty hopeless."

Fiona toyed with her napkin, then took a sip of water. "Nothing's hopeless, Jeremy." A happy twinkle lit up her eyes. "I got into the Academy of Ballet Arts today. Eleven A.M. professional class, starting next week."

"You went to the tryouts after all that?" Jeremy whistled under his breath. "You're something else." Then a shadow crossed his face. "But Fiona, what if it doesn't work again? What if you don't make it into a company?"

She had thought about that all morning on the way to the dance school. She knew the answer even before she had walked up the stairs into the narrow studio and introduced herself to the teacher. "I'll try another company. And another. And another. I'll survive."

Jeremy studied his sister's face. "You really mean that, don't you?"

"You bet!" Fiona declared. "And you'd better stop worrying about me. Whatever happens, I'll manage. I'm a big girl now, Jeremy. I'll get by."

She reached across the table and affectionately tugged his hair. "Hey, big brother. You know what the *real* problem is, don't you?"

Jeremy shook his head.

"We just don't know each other very well," Fiona admitted. "We've never had the chance until now."

As Jeremy contemplated his sister, a smile lit up his face. "Better late than never, mate!" He stirred his Coke with a straw, and didn't meet his sister's eyes as he said, "For instance, I now know never to set you up on a football date again."

Fiona felt a tug at the back of her throat. "Yes," she said, "Please be sure you don't do that again."

"Something's wrong between you and Jonathan?" Jeremy asked, his voice full of concern.

Fiona resisted the impulse to confide in her brother. She didn't want to talk to anyone about Jonathan not turning up after the rehearsal this afternoon, not kissing her good-bye earlier. "Jeremy, that's something else you have to learn — mind your own business," she joked. "But since you asked, I don't know if something's wrong." Her voice sank to a whisper. "I just don't know."

# Chapter
## 20

Opening night Fiona sat in the girls' dressing room, her nose buried in a huge bouquet of spring flowers. In the middle of the bouquet was a single red rose. Fiona pulled out the gorgeous rose and tucked it into her hair. She pulled up her tights and dabbed some glue on the heel of each foot before slipping on her ballet shoes. Then she read the note that came with the flowers one last time: *To the Best, Wishing You the Best*. The note wasn't signed but she recognized Jeremy's spidery handwriting. Fiona sighed. She had hoped the bouquet was from Jonathan.

Since Tuesday morning she hadn't seen him at all, not on the quad, not in the cafeteria, not even around the halls. He hadn't called, either. It was obvious he wanted to avoid her. He had talked Fiona into apologizing to the cast not because he cared about her, but because of his Holiday

Homeless Drive. Now that the show was salvaged, he probably never wanted to talk to her again. Fiona didn't blame him. She had been pretty stubborn and self-centered, and so completely blind to what she was doing. Jonathan had opened her eyes. Fiona was grateful for that. The problem was, she'd never have a chance to tell him now. Just like she'd never have a chance to tell him that she loved him. But she couldn't think about Jonathan now. Not until the final curtain came down, the cast party was over and she was finally home in bed.

A peal of laughter floated down the long narrow room. Fiona looked up and spotted Phoebe in her unzipped dress, Elise in her lopsided wig, and a host of other problems that Janie — who was helping the girls dress — would never have time to get to. Fiona sprang to her feet and got to work just as Woody shouted "Five minutes to curtain."

For Fiona's sake, Dee kept her fingers crossed during the whole first part of the show. "Please let it go well, without one single hitch," she had prayed. Fiona had come through her problems with the cast, and Dee was proud of her. So far, Dee's prayers had been answered. Now Elise Hammond was prancing across the stage, confiding in Phoebe that she was a girl who can't say no. Elise's vivacious, lively style had the audience in stitches. Elise looked ridiculous in her blonde wig, big pink hair ribbon, and banana curls bouncing with every exuberant step. She kicked her leg up in the air, revealing a pair of long pink ruffled bloomers but while she was singing, disaster struck. The wig slipped down over her face. At first, the audience was stunned. Then peals of laughter broke out across the auditorium. Michael kept the music going, but Elise stopped to yank off the wig. She stared at the handful of golden curly hair. Suddenly, a wicked look of inspiration crossed her face. Elise started to sing again, and at the closing line she hurled the wig, bow and all, across the orchestra pit into the front row. It landed right in Ted Mason's lap.

Ted jumped up and displayed his prize to the wildly applauding audience. Dee laughed uncontrollably before a wave of guilt washed over her. She sank down in her seat. Fiona was going to die.

The last note of the final production number crashed to a close. The curtain fell. Fiona held her pose one long second, then was aware of the whole cast cheering. She found herself face-to-face with Elise.

"You were wonderful," Fiona screamed, throwing her arms around the frightened girl. "I never saw anything so funny in my life." Fiona dissolved in giggles.

"That's show biz. You made the show, Elise," Woody laughed.

"With a little help from my friends," she smiled at Fiona.

Suddenly everyone was hugging and kissing. Someone tossed Fiona a towel. She dabbed the beads of sweat off her face.

"Curtain's going up," Woody shouted. Fiona felt Woody's big warm hand close on one of hers; Phoebe's on the other. Together, they all marched forward in front of the cast. Fiona's cheeks flushed with pride. She let go of Woody's hand and pushed him a couple of steps forward. Then she turned, faced the cast, and curtsied. Woody took his cue and bowed. The audience went wild.

Fiona, Phoebe, Bart, Elise, and Woody all stepped forward one more time. Fiona smiled over the footlights at Dee's cheers and Jeremy's whistles. She shaded her eyes and grinned at the front two rows. Front-row center, clapping, stamping, cheering like a raving lunatic, Jonathan Preston towered over everyone. The whole time, his eyes were fixed on her. Fiona sank into a deep bow and blew a kiss out to the audience, aiming directly at Jonathan. Then the curtain came down.

Woody whooped, and threw his arms around her. "We did it!" he screamed. "We really did it." Bart plucked her from Woody and spun her around and around. Someone shouted "Time for another bow!" from the wings. Fiona quickly smoothed her hair and got back into her position. The curtain came up. Her eyes once again sought Jonathan's. Fiona's smile froze . . . he was gone.

# Chapter
## 21

Fiona slipped out the back door of Michael Rifkin's house and made her way to the bus stop. It was late, but the number 10 ran all night, right down to Georgetown, to Garfield House. She leaned against the Plexiglas walls of the shelter and shivered. She looked back longingly at the figures silhouetted against the lit windows of Michael's mother's music room. Show music drifted out across the frozen lawn. The cast party would probably go on for hours. It was such a wonderful, crazy party. Half of Kennedy had turned up on Michael's doorstep, including a bunch of freshmen girls with flowers for Bart. The crowd would never let him live it down. As Ted Mason said, leave it to Bart to collect fans.

Part of Fiona had hated leaving. She hated breaking the warm bond that had developed between her and the cast ever since that horrible rehearsal. In all her years at Kingsmont she had never felt this connected to her friends. And they'd still be her close friends when the party was over, even though the show was done. Fiona smiled at the thought. Tonight had been almost perfect. It could have been if Jonathan hadn't pulled his vanishing act.

When the bus came, Fiona climbed inside and sat near a window. She had hoped Jonathan would turn up at the Rifkins'. When he didn't, Fiona knew her worst fears were coming true. Jonathan didn't want to be with her anymore. She had put on a brave, smiling face and danced with absolutely everybody. Then, when she couldn't stand it anymore, she slipped into the kitchen to leave by the back door and go home. But Chris and Greg were in the kitchen. Chris was feeding Greg some ice cream. Fiona overheard them talking about Garfield House and Brenda, and how she had run off with Jonathan and Matt Jacobs before the final curtain. Fiona didn't stay to hear more. She didn't know if Jonathan still loved her, but now she knew where to find him. Fiona had to tell him exactly how she felt: about the show, about herself, about him.

Fiona knocked on the front door of Garfield House. A short, brawny dark-haired man opened it. His sleeveless sweatshirt showed off a set of overdeveloped muscles but his dark eyes were warm and kind, and Fiona liked him instantly. He looked at Fiona a second, taking in her sequin-studded sneakers, sparkly tights, and short pink leather skirt. Then he stuck out his hand. "Welcome to Garfield House," he said in a slight Spanish accent. "I'm Tony Martinez. You don't have to tell me your name right away if you don't want to." He beckoned for her to follow him into the hall.

"Uh — I'm Fiona Stone," she said shyly. "I'm looking for Jonathan. Jonathan Preston. Is he here somewhere?" She looked around the narrow hall. Off to the left was a kind of living room. Some kids were sprawled on the rug in front of a TV munching popcorn and watching "The Honeymooners." Jonathan wasn't there.

Tony surprised her with a loud laugh. "Sorry, I took you for a runaway. You're from Kennedy High? You came here to help tonight?" Again he looked at her clothes.

"Runaway?" Fiona repeated. "No. I came right from the show," she said, self-consciously smoothing her skirt.

Tony led Fiona to the back stairs. "Down there. Follow the noise and you'll find Jonathan at the other end. I've got a kid in my office right now, or I'd show you the way." He smiled and left Fiona at the head of the stairs.

She crept down the creaky steps to the basement. By the time she reached the bottom, the din was overwhelming. So was the sight that met Fiona's eyes. She had expected a serious, quiet group of kids earnestly stacking cans in neat piles, or ironing shirts. Instead, the Fix-It club looked like it was hosting a huge bash. Bruce Springsteen's gravelly voice blared from the stereo. Some kids were dancing as they folded clothes. A chain of boys were making a game of tossing cans to each other before stashing them on tall, unpainted wooden shelves.

Brenda Austin was in a corner stuffing clothes into a huge white bin. Beside her was a good-looking guy Fiona didn't recognize, wearing old work clothes and carrying a clipboard. Next to him was Jonathan.

When she saw him, Fiona almost bolted back up the stairs. Everything she had wanted to tell him now seemed pointless. He looked so happy, so at home here, working side-by-side with his friends. But she wanted so badly to be near him.

As she stepped into the room, Brenda looked up and waved. Jonathan turned around. "Fiona," he cried. He crossed the basement in three long strides, and a second later she was in his arms.

"Jonathan," she whispered into his chest. She wrapped her arms tightly around his neck. She was so afraid he would vanish again.

He backed up from her slightly, so he could study her face. "I saw you wore my flower," he said.

"Your flower?" Fiona touched her hair. She had forgotten about the rose. A brown-edged petal drifted down onto the floor. Fiona stooped down and picked up the petal. She tucked it in her jacket pocket. "I thought the flowers were from Jeremy."

"Most were, but the rose was mine. I thought you knew."

"Maybe, somehow, I did," she whispered,

fingering the lapel of his jacket. Jonathan took her hand and kissed each finger. Then he seemed to remember where they were. He guided her behind the stairs, and pulled her down next to him on the old lumpy couch. In spite of the noise it was very private. Fiona gazed into his gray eyes, and felt as if she suddenly could see to the bottom of his soul. She reached up and touched his face. Her long, slender fingers traced the strong outline of his jaw, then his ear. She ran her hand down the back of his neck. His skin was surprisingly smooth, his hair almost silky. Fiona could hear her heart pounding even over the deep bass of a heavy metal band. She had the most incredible desire to kiss him and never stop.

"I was so afraid I ruined everything," she said softly, pressing her forehead against his chest.

"But it all worked out fine, Fiona."

Fiona shook her head. "I don't mean the show."

"Neither do I," Jonathan said, looking at her straight in the eye. "Neither do I."

Fiona's worried face relaxed into a soft smile. "You mean you forgive me for being such a creep at the football game?"

Jonathan arched his eyebrows. "No."

Fiona grew pale.

"I don't forgive you for being angry all the time, either, or calling my car names, or insulting my mechanical abilities, or acting like an A-Number-One snob on occasion to all our friends, or for having such a meddling big brother."

Fiona frowned and got up from the sofa.

"But, Fiona," Jonathan shoved his old hat back on his head, and stood up. "I love you, anyway," he said, a smile on his face as he towered over her. The next minute he had her in his arms again, and he spun her around and around and around the narrow space at the foot of the stairs.

"Hey, Preston, you're supposed to be working, not dancing," Matt Jacobs ribbed him from across the room.

But Jonathan didn't hear. His lips had found Fiona's and he couldn't tell exactly where their dance ended and their kiss began.

## Couples #18
*KISS AND RUN*

Elise stole a quick look at Ben; this tall, handsome boy who suddenly seemed like someone brand-new to her. Maybe she didn't want to go back to those childish days, she thought. Maybe the present could be every bit as interesting, in its own different way. . . .

"That's strange," Ben said nonchalantly. "We seem to be under the mistletoe, Elise."

"How did we get here?" she wondered out loud.

Ben shrugged mysteriously. "Can't imagine. But since we are here, we have to abide by the rules of the party."

A tight knot of apprehension grew in Elise's stomach. She could feel the heat rising in her cheeks.

"Yes, we have to, I guess. . . ."

Ben placed his two strong hands across her shoulders. He didn't hurry into the kiss. He

186

waited, with almost unbearable patience, until at last it was Elise who stood up on tiptoe and moved closer to him.

But it was Ben who claimed the kiss in the end. He was firm and confident. Once again Elise found herself responding with a fervor she'd never felt before. Her arms moved by themselves, it seemed, going up to encircle Ben's neck. When Ben finally lifted his head, she was breathless and wide-eyed.

"Ben . . ." she whispered in total surprise.

"Sshh." A feather-light kiss touched her brow before his lips moved slowly down along the curve of her cheek. His mouth closed over hers again in a kiss that drove away all thoughts of talk.

Elise felt something stirring inside her that made her feel certain she was falling in love with Ben. And, if she was reading the signs correctly, it seemed that her feelings were reciprocated.

"I can't believe this, Ben," she said in a trembling whisper. She felt like a mass of raw nerve endings, with every inch of her body tingling. She felt flushed and light-headed, dizzy with love. Why hadn't the possibility ever occurred to her before? Ben was wonderful. Well, this was a different Ben, one she didn't know quite so well yet, but he was no stranger.